The Wreath-Ribbon Quilt

The Wreath-Ribbon Quilt

by Ruth Moose

August House / *Little Rock*
PUBLISHERS

Published by August House, Inc.,
P. O. Box 3223, Little Rock, Arkansas, 72203,
501-663-7300.

Printed in the United States of America

10 9 8 7 6 5 4 3 2 1

LIBRARY OF CONGRESS CATALOGING-IN-PUBLICATION DATA
Moose, Ruth.
The wreath-ribbon quilt.
"Previously published by St. Andrews Press
in 1987"—T.p. verso.
1. Women—Southern States—Fiction.
I. Title.
PS3563.069W7 1989   813'.54   88-34412
ISBN 0-87483-084-2 (alk. paper)

First August House Edition, 1989

This book was previously published by St. Andrews Press in
1987.

Cover illustration by Byron Taylor
Production artwork by Ira Hocut
Typography by Lettergraphics, Memphis, Tennessee
Design direction by Ted Parkhurst
Project direction by Hope Norman Coulter

This book is printed on archival-quality paper which meets
the guidelines for performance and durability of the
Committee on Production Guidelines for Book Longevity of
the Council on Library Resources.

AUGUST HOUSE, INC.   PUBLISHERS   LITTLE ROCK

To the M and M's in my life, and others;
they know who they are.

Contents

Biography in Seven Lives

I Am Fifteen

THE BOY I hold would like to do other things, but he is the wrong sign in the wrong moon. However, we kiss a lot. He has not discovered breath mints and his tongue tastes of salt and burlap. The next time he calls, I say I'm busy. Then I stop answering the phone. Later I drive past his house at strange hours with strange friends. We honk the horn. Who lives there? they ask. I tell them I don't know. His father stands in the doorway in an undershirt. He wears a hat, black, round as a chocolate cake. He waves his fist. We sail away, folded in laughter.

At Seventeen

Someone has given me an ankle bracelet. I wear it in a green ring around my foot. I paint my toenails purple, smoke cigarettes in bathrooms and back seats, drink gin from paper cups, throw up beside the lake where lovers park.

At Nineteen

I marry in a white lace dress. It has a train six yards long. My mother tells her friends, *Six yards*. Her voice in all caps. To me she says, Are you sure this is what you want? I am not sure, but she has given me all the advice I can take. Does it have to be him? I don't know. He likes my laugh, the way I say things when I'm mad, how I look with moonlight washing my face and hair.

We drive a car decorated with words and streamers. Honeymoon Special. Rocks rattle in our hubcaps. We don't care. We'll have one night in a motel. I undress in the bathroom. He undresses in the bathroom. All my clothes are new. The labels scratch. I miss my old robe with its soft, sagging pockets. I miss my room where even in darkness I knew what hung on the walls. I miss the books I read in bed, left stacked like a ladder on each side.

We brush our teeth together, make faces in the mirror. Look, Ma. We read aloud from the one book we brought, an illustrated blue paperback; it tells all we need to know. This is what the doctor said, the one who gave us blood tests, sold us this book from his bottom drawer. He wanted me to take off my blouse so he could take my blood. I pushed up my sleeve, very high, very tight.

In bed, we study all the pages, words under the pictures. Are you *sure?* we say. We touch and giggle. What is this? How is it spelled?

After we turn out the lights, we tell ghost stories, play "the dead man game." His scrotum feels heavy and cool as a bunch of refrigerated grapes. Later he sleeps. I listen to trains in the night, a soft rain.

Next morning there is a stain where we slept. We leave holding hands, sharing secrets.

At Twenty-One

I have a job in a brown bank building without windows. I make roads of winding tapes for that great corporation. The numbers are a language all their own. I cannot speak it and all day must listen to their screams. At lunch, I escape. I run eight blocks to the steamy cafeteria, eat quickly, drift slowly back. I memorize department store windows, all the prices on drugstore specials. I let it rain on my face, snow on my nose, anything I can feel. Anything but the brown bank that sucks away my life.

A fruit vendor sits in an alley. I buy oranges, apples, grapes, one day a pear. He speaks no English, polishes perfect fruit shiny enough for a painting. One day he says, We mekka beautiful baby, no? I no longer buy the fruit but walk two blocks to avoid his alley.

When the baby is born, my mother says, Why couldn't you have waited? Did you do this to stop working?

My husband wanted a girl. I love my son, take him for long walks, show him the sky, trees, birds in many colors.

My husband hates his job. He comes home and yells things, pounds the table, rocks coffee in his cup, makes the baby cry. His sleep is a mix of snores and angry phrases. One day he wrecks the car. After, he has to take the bus to work. We try to save.

I push the baby in his stroller everywhere. We walk in rain and snow. If I stopped, we'd be statues. Pigeons would find us frozen, frost masks on our faces. Headlines herald Mother and Child Frozen in Park. Human popsicles. Eggs in my market basket turned to marble. I learn to knit. A friend teaches me over tea. Camomile. We share the same bag. She likes lime juice, but I eat the wedge from lemon rind. I learn to heel perfectly, make a matching pair. I knit all the time; my goal, a pair of socks. Blue, wool, size Men's. The first time he wears them, he says they itch. I wash the socks in very lovely hot water, spin them dry, and they are mine. I deserved them from the first.

I learn to make good spaghetti. And fruitcakes. I make shining wreaths of them for friends.

The baby grows. On his second birthday he reaches for the cake, breathes out the candles that sputter in the wind.

My husband sits on the floor, asks, Are you happy?

I cry at the sink, dishes stacked gray as oysters' shells beside my salty sea.

Would you like another baby?

I cry louder. Great rocking waves.

He goes out, comes home with a cactus in a red plastic pot. He puts it in the bedroom. The plant hates me. It sprays stickers when I get near. One day, in counterattack, I spray it with sweet and flower-smelling starch. Pffft. It coughs. A year later, dies.

I do not get pregnant. No one has invented the Pill, but someone thought of other things. I thank them with all my heart and soul and with all my other things.

My husband puts a fence around the back yard. I plant a garden. Lettuce and onions. Also mint, thyme, radishes, roses. I lean my face into them, inhale their air, crush them between my fingers, tuck sprigs in my pillow for dreams. A morning glory grows around my doorstep, climbs gutters, blooms in my face. Its blue trumpets say things only I know are true. When frost blackens it, I cry, hold the dead hearts in my hand, curl the dry vines like hair around my fingers.

In summer we sit on the porch, cut the baby's hair. He looks like a young midget, sad and scared. His eyes are dark, deep, absorbing as a priest.

Silly, my husband says, it will grow back.

At Twenty-Four

My husband gets another job in another town and we move. Every night we put the baby to bed, then walk around boxes. We pack and pack. I say goodbye to neighbors I never knew. We'll miss you, they sing. I'll miss morning glories, the silent, wise sayings. They will be back, but not me. I leave aphids on the rosebushes. They will have to be taught to trellis by someone else. Will she know? Will she call them by name? Learn their special ways? I want to leave instructions, a list. Don't, my husband says, it will only get lost. I tape it inside a cabinet door, shut tight.

In the new town, I join clubs, go to meetings, play dress-up, guess who I am.

We have another baby. This time I do not cry. She is a happy child. Fat as a pumpkin, smiling like a jack-o'-lantern.

I walk her in sunshine. We make valentines together, cut out cookies, plan parties, play games. I Spy and Animal, Vegetable, or Man?

We join Brownie Scouts, learn things. Where man began, why dinosaurs died, how woman was made. We ask questions of the plastic parts, study the fine wire tuning, the empty head.

At Thirty-Five

I go back to school, sit in a class with long-haired boys who wear leather bracelets, smell of soap and spice, collect sugar in their beards. I paint large canvases I must have help to carry to the car, to our apartment with no one home but the cat, Arthur.

One weekend I join a group of sisters, a pajama party, a one-day boarding school. I wake in a row of beds, we eat crackers, drink ginger ale, juice. Practice walking the line until we are steady enough to leave. For a week I bleed babies, my egg basket empty. Coward, I call my husband, a vasectomy is so simple.

Simple to you, he says, not so simple to me.

He is forty-five and hates his job. It isn't going anywhere. He isn't going anywhere. Do you want to be like this when you are sixty-five? he asks. His friends from the rat race drop by the wayside. We wire flowers, send job resumés by mail.

Teaching, he says, is the answer. He has never taught before, but an overzealous administrator thinks he can. They give him chalk, a roll book and pen. He whistles in the shower. After three months of teaching, they reprimand. Conduct unbecoming a man of the faculty. A student shed her woes on his shoulder four noons in a row.

At Forty

We move to the woods, build a house on ten acres of rock. No one in his right mind would live here, a forest ranger claims. At last we found the place, my husband says.

A creek tumbles by our doorstep, but we drill 465 granite feet to find water. The bit churns gray grit like a core to the middle of the earth. We pay by the foot. I expect oil, or at least vintage champagne.

The water, when it comes, is urine-yellow, tastes of rust and month-old eggs. Minerals, my husband says, we can bottle and sell it.

I cut trees, grow strong, a Paula Bunyon. My daughter and I clear Wonder Woman Corner. She says a woman should not be forced to work this way. It is not becoming. Her friends ride in cars, go to dances, eat pizza. She runs away with the lightning rod salesman. No rod he sold has ever been hit. He gives no guarantees. Drives a red Mustang with dice dancing above the dash.

I find my son in the closet kissing the Avon lady. She is fifteen, dressed in blue. Her hat and satchel match. Her legs in fringed short jeans match. It's our latest shade, she says. Would you care for a sample?

Are you sure? I ask my son. Is she the one?

One? he says. What is one? They leave in a van with double bumper stickers. The front says, "Opera Lives" and "Save Our Ballet." The rear reads, "Preserve Wildlife. Kill Hunters."

They cross the bridge, don't look back.

I wave. My hand feels hinged at the wrist.

Do you know what it's like, my husband says, to go in *cold?* To ask for work from strangers? Make appointments? To write these letters no one ever answers?

The game warden drives a green car. He has a red beard that shines like sunset, smells of fields, tickles like moss. The hair on his arms and chest is fine gold wire. I curl it in my fingers, kiss it in my sleep. While my husband hunts for work, the game warden comes. I let down my hair. We swim in the lake. Are you in charge of fish? I ask. He laughs like the mating call of some rare bird, chases me through woods to a pine-needle bed. Won't someone see? I ask. Who? He breathes sweet into my neck. Who? An owl during the day. I am filled with clouds and sky and leaves of green, green, green. An old song, a tune I've hummed along the years. Today I shout my name.

Moon Over Magnolias

SOME WOMEN, WHEN they were pregnant, went to museums and art galleries; Annabelle Givens went to church. In her seventh month, for some unknown reason, she began to be drawn to churches: brick, colonial churches, graystone red-doored cathedrals, a blue-domed mosque, white-steepled clapboards. Every time she passed a church, Annabelle imagined herself sitting in the congregation, preferably under a stained glass window, the sun streaming through a radiant madonna with child. The background was always blue with both clouds and stars.

Annabelle first tried a church two blocks from their apartment. One Sunday morning she put on her pink gingham, combed her long, dark hair and tied it back with a pink scarf. She felt like a six-year-old going to school the first day and that perhaps she ought to skip her feet, but that would bounce this basketball she wore where her stomach used to be. She brushed her hair, pulled two tendrils over her ears and thought wistfully of a straw hat she'd worn as a child. A wide sailor with navy velvet ribbon that streamed down the back, held on with a thin rubber band that cut into her chin. She'd chewed it in two once listening to her grandfather, black-suited and white-shirted in the pulpit, holding his gold watch on a chain and calling on God to "lead them in the paths of righteousness." Annabelle thought that was the longest hour in the world. It was a week long—forever, but she sat quietly in that garden of hats and flowers. Her grandmother's hats had veils and silk roses. She sat quietly as prayer in that small Southern church of blue-green windows where piano notes drifted out and a yellow jacket or bee drifted in to be blessed. Somehow Annabelle felt she ought to wear gloves or at least carry them, but they went out with hats. Besides it was too hot. She snapped shut her flat leather purse and started out.

Richard lifted an eyebrow over his newspaper as she walked past.

"I'm going to church," she said. "The white one on the corner."

"Okay," he said, refolding the sports section, then stopped and looked at her. "Are you all right?"

"I'm fine," she said. "I'm just going to church."

He shook his head and gave her a little corner of a smile that said she was subject to whims "in her condition." That Victorian phrase. She read it in his eyes. "Her condition" was her own choice and she'd waited a long time for it and she was enjoying it—most of the time. She didn't enjoy the twinges in her back, nor feeling like Humpty Dumpty, not being able to see her toes . . . but she did like feeling for the first time that her body could do wonderful things, she was a special person doing something only she could do. Which wasn't altogether true. She had to give Richard a little credit. But after that the rest had been up to her—body and mind.

She walked slowly, sunshine on her forehead, warm on her shoulders, past two blocks of apartments identical to theirs except for an occasional plant in a window, watching cat, bird cage, or twirling mobile of gulls or boats or shells. Still she was early. There were only two elderly men inside the darkened vestibule. The tall one reminded her of Richard's Uncle Harry. The other had a bald spot the size of a quarter that shined as he bent to hand her a bulletin.

She eased into a rear pew. The organist started chimes and bells, "Sweet Hour of Prayer," and a few people drifted in, seated themselves. Annabelle was surprised she recognized the music. And pleased. She admired the polished wooden pews, the altar arrangement of orange spiked-flowers and white chrysanthemums big as salad plates.

Two women took seats in front of her, continued their conversation. The younger one in black linen, too-red hair and thick make-up wore a heavy perfume that reminded Annabelle of the time she was three and poured her mother's perfume down the front of her dress, emptying the whole bottle. She had been promptly popped in the tub and scrubbed, soaked, and shampooed. Annabelle coughed. Magnolias. She hated them. "Dusky Magnolias" had been the perfume. Her mother never wore it again and even the word became a family joke. Anyone put down was said to have been "magnoliaed." Her father, dousing the neighbor's persistent dog on the boxwoods with the garden hose, laughed that he "magnoliaed Pee Wee."

The woman in black said to her friend, "I've only been there once. I don't care for that kind of music, but I'm forty-seven and still single so I think it's about time I started looking seriously—don't you?"

The woman nodded.

"Even though I don't think I look it—forty-seven, I mean. Do you?"

She went on without waiting for an answer. "No one would know if I didn't tell them." She fanned with one of the hymnals, flapping its cover with a slapping sound. "This is the hottest place in the church. I've told that sexton the air conditioner doesn't reach back here and I don't think he's even tried."

She swiveled in her seat, said to Annabelle, "Are you a member here? Who are you?"

Annabelle opened her mouth but the woman went on.

"I've been here over thirty years and I've never seen you before."

Annabelle felt herself being inspected like a cake in a bakery window, sides, top, and all around the edges.

"I'm—" she started, but the organ swelled suddenly and the choir filed in. She almost said "Magnolia."

After the service, Annabelle signed the Friendship Register: name, address, member of this church. She checked No. Would like a visit from the minister. She checked No!

Next Sunday she tried the graystone church. No one there asked her name, but the minister looked like Robert Redford in a black robe with yellow satin cowl. She put him in a cowboy hat on a prairie with a changing sunset behind, then a canyon and a river. He had great flowing sleeves and dramatic movements with his arms that seemed to Annabelle he might scoop up all the congregation and suddenly lift off toward the skies. He preached sermons on responsibilities to earth, keepers of the here and now, caretakers for the future, our children's children's children. She liked that and that was the church she chose.

Richard didn't understand, but each Sunday he cleared away the breakfast clutter, grapefruit shells, waffle batter, and honey pitcher. When she returned, he had things marinating for dinner. One Sunday he made sourdough bread from starter his brother had given them. Annabelle might be concerned about spirit, but Richard wanted to make sure there was bread.

"If you're worried about something," Richard said one Sunday, kneading the dough with both hands, rocking it back and forth, "we can talk about it."

"No." She untied her hair, fluffed it out. "I'm fine. Really."

He kissed the back of her neck smelling of wheat and earth, left a flour smudge on her cheek.

She was a little tired. For the past several nights she hadn't been sleeping well. The baby woke her in the early morning hours, restless, kicking, thumping inside like an acrobat. He (she'd called the baby that since the first hard kick—future quarterback's toe, she was sure) wasn't going to be the sleeper his father was. Richard lay beside her sleeping deep as a rock. She rose and walked to the window, gazed across the back lawn. Everything was silver, softly dusted in powdered silver. Moonlight. Too beautiful to waste on sleep. She'd always felt that way. As a child she often walked the house at night, listening, looking out, touching things. Everything was different at night. Her mother called her a moon child, a night-blooming cereus. A flower that bloomed at night. One summer Annabelle stayed up all night in her mother's garden watching the cereus open, her sleeping bag in the swing, with a flashlight and her Raggedy Ann, whose button eyes saw everything Annabelle did.

Annabelle wondered now if her baby would be another moon child? She thought of him now swimming in darkness, eyes shut tightly as a kitten's, swimming and kicking.

She drank a glass of cold milk standing in the light from the refrigerator. Richard stood in the doorway, rubbed his sleep-twisted hair. "What's wrong?"

"Nothing," Annabelle said, "the baby woke me. Kicking."

Richard rubbed her stomach. "I'm sorry," he said.

"I'm not," she said. "I'm excited and happy and exhilarated and everything but sleepy." She reached both arms around his waist, buried her head against his warm chest, listened to the steady knock of his heart. They walked back to bed, arms around each other.

"I used to carry you," Richard said.

"Give me a rain check on that," she said and was asleep within minutes after slipping between the sheets.

Two weeks before her due date—it almost glowed in neon on the calendar to Annabelle—she decided to give herself a home permanent. The instructions on the box sounded so simple. Ten Easy Steps to a New You and a Lot of Body Without Curl. Or curls galore. She had a lot of body—oh boy, did she—what she'd like was a little curl.

While Richard watched Monday night football, Annabelle got out scissors, timer, towels, cotton, curlers—a rainbow-hued box of them in six different sizes. She shampooed and started winding. No odor, no mess, the box promised, but her fingers kept slipping and her eyes smarted. She wore a pair of old black maternity shorts and one of Richard's holey T-shirts. "Make Love, Not War" printed on the back, but the "War" was almost faded off.

When she finished she was a walking beachball with a wreath of curlers, her crown of plastic. She twisted on the plastic turban, waded past towels and cotton and misspent end papers, timer in hand, to the screened porch.

There she sat cooling herself amid plants and record jackets, books and milk-carton crate furniture. At this point, Annabelle had discovered the only comfortable chair in the house was a folding canvas one. She fitted into it as if the chair had been made to fit—there wasn't an inch wasted. She was reading "Introduction to Motherhood" and didn't hear the bell. Only voices. Close. She looked up from her magazine to see Richard and the two women from church, who stared at her. "We're from the visiting committee," one said.

"What?" Annabelle, startled, tried to get up, only to find she'd outgrown this chair and it wasn't going to let her go. The chair rose a few inches with her, before she sank back down.

"Church," the woman said. "St. Marks."

"But I checked—" Annabelle started.

Richard offered the ladies seats on the daybed they used for a sofa. He gave them pillows from the stack on the floor and they accepted them eagerly, tucked and pummeled them behind their backs. Then he disappeared after they said a glass of iced tea would "just save their lives at this moment." They were "perishing."

"We usually call first," the woman in a blue print polyester said. "But we were in the neighborhood and saw your lights and I said, Carolina, let's just drop in. We won't stay but a second. Just to say we've been and can put it on our card."

I'll kill Richard, Annabelle thought. How could he do this? She struggled to make her lips form even a tight little smile. Of all the times . . . she tugged down her T-shirt, reached toward her plastic-wrapped head.

"We've been out since four this afternoon," Mrs. Green Shirtwaist said, running her fingers inside her belt. "And we haven't even introduced ourselves," she giggled. "I'm Carolina Stout and this is Evelyn Love. I bring you love, I tell people." She poked Evelyn, who beamed.

"I'm in the middle—" Annabelle held out her timer.

"Of course you are, dear," said Carolina, "and my, don't you look cool? That's important at a time like this. I planned my babies so they'd be born in the winter and I wouldn't have to suffer so during the hot weather. I do suffer so with the heat, don't you, Evelyn?" She turned to her friend, who had pinched off the tops of four avocado pits Annabelle sprouted.

"If you don't do that, honey," Evelyn said, "they just run to the ceiling and you have nothing but stalk. I know. I used to run a nursery, didn't I, Carolina?"

"She's done the flowers for St. Mark's for over twenty years. You ought to see her cross of white lilies at Easter," Carolina said. "With little lights and all."

When Annabelle's timer rang both women jumped, put their hands to their chest. "Goodness gracious, that startled me."

"I have to do the next step," Annabelle stood, this time without the chair. "Now if you'll excuse me." She'd planned to check a test curl in thirty minutes, now it had been forty. She had to hurry. Where was Richard? She yelled, louder than she meant to—and noticed the women exchange glances.

Richard came from the kitchen balancing a tray with two tall glasses, napkins, a dish of sliced lemons, even a sprig of the mint that had overtaken her salad garden. "I couldn't find the iced tea spoons," he said.

She dashed to the bathroom, unwinding curlers as she went. Who cared if all the curls came out—it would be better than a tangled Brillo-pad mass of them.

She heard Richard showing the ladies out as she worked the neutralizer through her hair. Curls. She had thousands of curls, each demanding to stand up—out—in an individual way. But she wasn't going to cry. Maybe it was supposed to look like this. She rinsed until the water ran cold, then reached for her rollers. Surely when she took it down, she would look like the picture in the folder. Easy. One, two, three, for the beauty shop look at home prices.

Richard was propped in bed reading when she finished. She had decided never to speak to him again. Their child would have to learn to talk early to tell Richard all she wanted to say. How could he have done such a thing?

"I couldn't help it," Richard said. "They just came in."

"You could have told them I was indisposed," she hissed.

"I've got a feeling typhoid wouldn't keep those two out," he mumbled.

She slept in his arms, not waking once. He left for the office without waking her.

The first thing she did was take down her hair, trembling. What if the permanent hadn't worked? All her work and worry for nothing. Each curl tumbled off its roller, squiggled out like a corkscrew, danced, looked alive. And she looked like Orphan Annie—a very pregnant Orphan Annie. Which wouldn't do at all. Maybe for another face at another time and place, but not her, not now. Her own baby wouldn't know her with all these curls that had curls. Magnoliaed, she saluted with her hairbrush, and a sigh.

Annabelle drove to the drop-in beauty salon where slim-hipped girls and guys in jeans snipped and aimed blow-dryers. "Cut." She made scissor motions with her fingers. "Off."

"Is this your first?" the beauty shop operator asked. "How much longer you got?" She measured Annabelle's girth, the chair, with her eyes.

"Permanent?" Annabelle said. "I hope not." Then the scissors flashed around her like a swarm of minnows. When she looked her hair lay like wood shavings on the floor and she felt pounds lighter. Someone with large eyes, bangs, and a gamin grin looked back from the mirror.

"It's you," the operator said. "The real you that's been inside trying to get out."

Annabelle laughed. Inside her was a real little person trying to get out.

She paid the girl, had brunch at the snack bar of an old-fashioned drugstore with a whirling wooden-bladed paddle fan.

Too early for her doctor's appointment, she walked through the park, sat on a shady green bench. Pigeons with purple and green necks strutted around her feet, pecked. She had nothing to feed them, not even a stale cracker in the far corners of her bag.

"That's okay." A bag lady of a woman wobbled up. "I bring bread every day. That's what they want."

The pigeons cooed and fluttered around her. Some sat on her head, shoulders, arms, as she pulled bread scraps from brown bags and fed them, called them by name. "June Bug, Pretty Boy, Dancing Girl . . . Lillie Marlane . . . Gigi . . . they know me," the old woman said.

Annabelle wanted to move but she was afraid she would hurt the woman's feelings. She wore a wool hat and sweater with the elbows out. It wasn't buttoned in front and you could see her slip, the color of burlap.

"When you due, honey?" the woman asked, petting a pigeon on her lap. She stroked its head like a cat and it gave purring coos.

"Two weeks," Annabelle said. "On the seventeenth."

"You won't go until the thirty-first," the woman said. "That's the full moon. I used to work in a hospital. I know." She folded her bag and tucked it inside her sweater, shuffled away.

A woman with a blonde ponytail and green slacks walked by pushing twins in a stroller. She smiled at Annabelle. The toddlers in matching sun hats clutched sand shovels and pails that rattled and clanked.

"One or two?" she asked Annabelle, who found she was cuddling her stomach.

"One," Annabelle said.

The woman laughed. "My mother always said I never did things the easy way. Good luck." She aimed the stroller toward the play area and started up again, the twins singing.

Annabelle followed and chose an empty swing, watched the congregation of mothers and children, fathers and children, a grandfather and children. In the distance she heard a carillon—or was it the ice cream vendor? Through the trees sun filtered like stained glass. Annabelle relaxed. She felt suddenly happy enough to shout, and inside, her moon child kicked and jumped.

To Banbury Cross

RILLA SAW HERSELF in the toes of her Sunday shoes: her saucer face, her long blonde hair, and Mama brushing. She wiggled her feet, the pictures blurred, disappeared.

"Sit still." Mama's hand capped Rilla's head. The brush smoothed down, scratched her neck and tickled.

"Let me do it." Rilla reached around.

"Not this time." Mama drew back the brush. "We're in a hurry."

"You hurt," Rilla said.

"I have to get the tangles out," Mama said, lifting Rilla's hair. The air was cool on her neck. "You don't want Daddy to see you with tangles in your hair."

"If you don't sit still"—Grandma spraddled like an old sawhorse before the tall dresser mirror—"and let your mama get the tangles out, birds will come build nests in your hair."

"I wish they would." Rilla cupped her hands, made a round place in her lap.

"Pshaaaa." Grandma made an ugly noise with her lips,

took a hat from a square gray box.

Birds nests in my hair, Rilla sang under her breath. Red birds, blue birds, squat. Birds would lay eggs and I can take them to the hospital. A present for Daddy. To make him feel better. Get well.

Grandma jammed the black knob of a hat on her head, jerked it off, pushed it on again.

Mama's fingers moved gently in Rilla's hair, the brush singing low noises. Whispers. Last night there were whispers after the patrolman left on his motorcycle. Daddy had a motorcycle that made loud hissing and popping sounds. The patrolman's motorcycle was quiet like his voice when he said Daddy was unconscious and nobody could find Mama. She was here with me, Rilla thought, here all the time. When Daddy came to, the patrolman said, he told them where Mama was. Came to what? The hospital? Unconscious was asleep, Mama said later, and not to worry Daddy was fine. Rilla didn't go back to sleep for a long time after that. She dreamed Daddy rode a bucking black horse, a wild horse. He kicked his sides and made him paw the air, blow smoke and fire from his nose. Daddy fell off and lay on the ground. Unconscious. Un-con-scious. Rilla puffed the words under her breath.

"Be still." Mama brushed a tangle.

"Ouch." Rilla's eyes stung.

Grandma jabbed a pearl-headed hat pin in her hat. "I've never in my life seen a youngun so tenderheaded." She made a face at the mirror.

Mama brushed harder. "We've got to hurry."

"If I was you, Merle"—Grandma powdered her neck and throat—"I'd cut that child's hair. Not put up with that fuss." Her powder puff made soft slaps, fluttered like something caught in her dress front. "If you'd cut her hair it would thicken up. I cut yours when you was little." She closed the powder box. "And you've had thick hair ever since. Thick as a horse's tail."

Rilla stuck out her tongue. "I don't want a horse's tail for hair."

Grandma picked up her purse, swung around.

Rilla quick-licked her lips with the angry tongue.

"I'd not lick my lips and go out in this wind." Grandma peered into her purse. "They'll chap quick."

The metal feet of Rilla's hairclasp scratched as Mama slid it into place, snapped it shut. Daddy liked her white bow hairclasps. Bows in her hair, he'd sing, bells on her toes. He said rhymes, made her laugh.

"You've got some natural curl." Mama patted Rilla's hair. "Not as much as your Daddy's, but some." She smoothed the back of her dress. "I wanted your hair to be black like his, not blonde and stringy like mine."

Rilla played with Daddy's hair when he slept on the couch, sometimes. Curling it over and under her fingers, ruffling it up and laying kisses in it.

"The baby's hair . . ." Mama started, then stopped, turned away.

Grandma's purse clicked shut. "Better hurry. I heard Mr. Ellis turn off the highway. He'll be here in a minute. He's mighty good to take us and we mustn't make him wait."

Rilla flung on her coat, started past Grandma.

"Wait," Mama called above the coat-hanger clatter. "You need your cap. Wait."

Rilla tried to dodge Grandma in the doorway.

"We'll put it on easy and not mess up your hair," Mama said.

"No." Rilla tried to go around the other side.

"Better put it on." Grandma grabbed her shoulder. "I don't want you keeping me awake half the night with another earache. I don't like to get up and heat sweet oil for little girls who won't wear their caps when they ought."

Please. Mama formed the word with her lips, *please.* Her fingers fumbled under Rilla's chin as they heard Mr. Ellis's car brakes squawk. Mr. Ellis parked his car in the barn, chickens roosted on it. He used it like a truck, the back seat out, drove out to the fields. Rilla had seen the car often on the hill, its trunk open like a hungry mouth and Mr. Ellis feeding it bale after bale of hay.

Mr. Ellis held the seat for Mama and Rilla to climb in back. "Cold enough for you?" He chewed, shifted the pouch in his jaw. "There was ice in my hog troughs this morning."

He had put a wooden chair in the car for Mama. Rilla stood until the car reached the highway, then climbed onto her mother's lap. It was good to sit on Mama's lap and not have Grandma say she was too big, that her mother wasn't strong and Rilla would break her down.

Mr. Ellis shot a brown stream, rolled up his window. "It looked like this winter was never going to get cold enough to do any hog killing. Craziest weather I've ever seen. Them hogs got fat and meaner every day." He shot again and brown dribbled the glass.

Through a hole in the floor, silver dollar–sized, Rilla watched the road flow under them. Sometimes there was a sparkle of glass, a bit of white.

Grandma droned in the front seat, ". . . fool on a motorsicle. I knowed before it happened. I said a hundred times when him and Merle was living with me, he was going to get himself killed. Bless pat, if he didn't near do it. I'll never know why the Lord saw fit to spare the likes of him"—she lowered her voice—"and him riding with . . ."

"That's enough, Ma," Mama said so sharply Rilla jumped, almost slid off her lap. "I don't want to hear another word."

Grandma sniffed, straightened her shoulders.

Rilla reached, brushed white flecks off her grandmother's shoulders.

Grandma jerked around, frowning. "What you doing?"

"Dandruff. You got dandruff, Grandma."

"No, I ain't." Grandma craned her neck, shook her collar. "More than likely it was lint."

Rilla waved to a greening willow tree. Mrs. Cranston at her mailbox waved back.

"Ma, Mrs. Cranston waved to you," Mama said.

"Law me and I wasn't looking," Grandma said. "She'll just have to think I'm stuck up if she wants, but I can't help I didn't see her till we was past."

Mr. Ellis said he had to get some wire from the FCX. As long as he was making a trip to town, he might as well get some use from it himself.

A brown and white dog charged the car, barking. Mr. Ellis hit his horn, swerved to the other side.

Grandma said he should have gone ahead and hit the thing. It would have been one less to worry about. That if people had to have dogs, they ought to be made to keep them shut up.

"How much longer?" Rilla's head itched under the cap. She pushed it back until the ties were choking tight.

"Not much." Mama adjusted the cap. "You may have to wait in the lobby. I don't know if you can go see Daddy or not."

"She most certainly can," Grandma snorted. "I'd not leave a child of mine in a strange lobby. No telling who might come along and take her off."

Rilla squeezed her mother's arm. "Can't I see Daddy?"

"It would be a lesson for her"—Grandma looked straight ahead—"something she won't forget."

"That's what worries me," Mama said. "It might give her nightmares."

Rilla stood, held the back of the seat. "No, it won't. I promise." How could Daddy give her nightmares? Mares were horses. Horses to ride in the dark. Daddy used to ride her on his knee, sing, "Ride a cock horse to Banbury Cross to see a fine lady upon . . ." That was when she was little. Later she rode behind him on the motorcycle, flew through the wind, her hair floated like ribbons. Don't go so fast, she screamed. Slow down. Her words came back, hit her face—fast, too fast. Daddy went too fast and had a wreck. He was in the hospital. "What's a lobby?"

"A room with chairs in it." Mama sounded tired. "A place people sit and wait."

They passed houses with fence-framed yards, curlicued front walks. We lived in a house with Daddy . . . before the baby died, when Mama still liked Daddy, before she cried so much. Grandma's house had a snaggle-tooth porch, nothing and nobody to play with. Only limp paper dolls cut from the Spiegel catalog.

Mr. Ellis stopped before the biggest building Rilla had ever seen. All glass and shiny posts, it seemed to have a thousand window eyes, a mouth that swallowed people. She tried to count the windows but tripped going up the walk, and Grandma said she better watch where she was going.

Inside, Rilla snatched off her ugly red cap, packed it in her pocket. Woodpecker cap Grandma knitted. When Rilla wore it she felt like going around pecking.

The lobby was filled with people, noise, and smelled funny. White like the doctor's office. Rilla pinched her nose together until it hurt.

They took stairs because Grandma said she didn't like elevators. "Don't want to be shut up in one of them things. If I'm going to be in a box, I want to be dead and not know it." The baby was dead, shut up in a box, and Grandma said it was all for the best.

Rilla liked to ride things. Did an elevator go up like the ponies on the merry-go-round at the fair? Daddy took her once, lifted her on a pony. It was fun. She waved to him every time she went past until his face wasn't there. When the pony stopped still and the music quit, a dirty man who smelled of liniment helped her down. Daddy was gone. She called to him, looked for his blue jacket with stars, the sign on the back. He was watching a lady dressed in pink feathers dance to a drum. Boom, boom. Rilla's feet went boom, boom on the stairs. Grandma's shoes clacked and Mama's high heels clicked.

Several times Rilla stopped, leaned over to look down.

Grandma grabbed her coattail. "You'll fall, bust your head wide open, if you don't watch out!"

Rilla could see her head in two neat watermelon halves, her thoughts like seeds arranged in rows. Red and juicy, some seeds would scatter, spill on the floor. She held the rail, walked carefully, not looking down.

"Shhh," Mama said in the hall. "Tiptoe. Sick people don't like noise. They'll make us leave."

Rilla tiptoed behind the nurse in her silky dress that whispered words she couldn't quite hear.

The nurse snapped on a light, said to a snow bank in the bed: "Mr. Lewis, you got company." Her voice was loud and Rilla wanted to turn her low. "Feel like waking up and talking to them?"

"Eugene!" Mama ran to the bed. A voice that didn't sound like Daddy said, "Merle, Merle, honey, I'm sorry. Sorry as I can be."

The nurse checked a chart, clipped her pen on a pocket. "He's a mighty lucky man and better take it easy for a few days."

Grandma stood behind the bed. "How you feeling, Gene?"

Daddy didn't look at her.

"Stiff and sore, I reckon." She opened a dresser drawer, slid in the paper bag she carried. "You'll be needing another pair of pajamas or two. These were Merle's father's, but you're welcome to them."

"Thanks," Daddy mumbled.

Mama sat on the edge of the bed, talking. Daddy kept saying he would give anything in this world if all this had never happened.

Grandma adjusted the blinds, straightened the curtains, unpinned a card from some green plants. "That was quick," she said, reading the card. "Ebenezer Baptist. They was good to bother to send anything." She moved the plants to face the sun. "No more than Gene ever saw fit to go."

Mama and Daddy held hands, talked.

"Of course it was for my sake. Longtime-member-in-good-standing." She poked the plants. "Haven't been watered in no telling when." She filled a glass in the bathroom, watered the plants, gave a vase of pink flowers a quick pour, as though they didn't deserve a drink since they would die anyway but she wanted to prove she was fair.

Sweet-smelling pink flowers in round rings stood on the grave when baby brother died. Grandma said his blood was bad and it was a wonder he lived two weeks. Gene's family had bad blood. Rilla had it too. Bad blood made her do mean things, hit the chicken with a hoe, break Grandma's tulips, lick spoons when nobody looked.

Grandma put the glass back. "You get well quick now, Gene."

Daddy closed his eyes, didn't move his swollen lips.

"Don't worry about a thing. Merle and Rilla are just fine with me."

Daddy opened one eye, looked at Mama. She was pale, her hair mussed.

"Jack Hunter said it was okay about those back bills." Grandma wiped her wet hands on the sheet.

Mr. Hunter's store had a dozen different kinds of candy and Daddy let Rilla pick out as many of every kind as she wanted, fill a bag until its sides were fat.

"He's waited two years to get his money." Grandma looked out the window. "Guess he can wait a while longer."

Mama filled her cheeks with air, her face got red. "Ma"— she stood quickly—"I thought you were going to see Martha Allen while we were here."

Grandma tugged her dress front, patted her hat and left.

Rilla sat under the bed, wiped dust from the slats. Her foot hit the stool and it slid with a screech.

"Rilla, honey"—Mama reached down—"I forgot all about you. Come give Daddy a kiss." She lifted her to the bed.

The man was not Daddy. His head was bandaged white, his beard gone. "No." Rilla pushed back. "No!" She tried to wiggle away, but Mama held her.

Daddy reached up, stroked her hair. It wasn't Daddy's hand, the nails were clean and white. Daddy had black nails, his hands smelled of grease. "How's my girl?" His lips were thick, blue. Only his eyes, dark and deep, were Daddy's eyes. "Don't let them cut your hair, you hear?" He kissed a twirling rope.

"No." Rilla kicked the bed and hurt her toe.

"Put her down, Merle," he said. "She's afraid, that's all. It's okay, baby."

Rilla buried her face in Mama's scratchy skirt.

"I guess I do look pretty bad," Daddy said.

Mama's skirt smelled of Grandma's closet, the block that hung there to kill brown butterflies.

"I wasn't going fast," Daddy said. "The needle hit sixty, I saw gravel." His hand played with the sheet. "And that's the last thing I saw."

Rilla curled in a chair in the corner.

"Flying through the air," Daddy said, "I felt that. It was the craziest feeling."

When I jump from the peach tree, Rilla thought, it feels like flying.

"Funny"—Daddy shaded his eyes—"I don't remember ever hitting the ground."

"Hush." Mama bent over him. "Let's not talk about it."

"What went with my bike?"

"The highway patrol has it—what's left." Mama fluffed his pillow. "They said it was a total loss." She kissed his forehead. "You're here and that's all that matters."

Total loss. Lost. I'll never get to ride the bike behind Daddy anymore.

A nurse bobbed her white cap in the doorway. "Time for all visitors to leave."

Tiptoeing, Rilla saw Grandma in the hall. She talked to a nurse behind a desk.

"You don't know what my daughter's been through. Merle has never been one to turn tail and run, but there's just so much a person can stand. I said it wouldn't work when she married him, but you can't tell young people a thing." Grandma leaned closer. "He's always been wild. I told him about that motorsicle."

"He sure was lucky." The nurse shook her head. "The girl with him was killed instantly."

Rilla froze. I'm not dead. I wasn't with Daddy. I wasn't

killed instantly. She toppled, caught herself against the cool wall. Mama never rode behind Daddy on the bike, just me.

Grandma stepped back when she saw Rilla, held her purse flat in front with both hands. "Where's your Mama? Is she coming?"

Rilla looked at her shoes.

Grandma turned to the nurse. "I walked clean to the seventh floor to see Martha Allen. She had gone for x-rays. I left a note I'd been. Don't want her going home, saying none of the neighbors come to see her."

Rilla spelled out the nurse's red badge: "M-R-S H-A-R-T."

The nurse stopped writing, smiled at her. "You're a smart little thing. How old are you?"

"I'm six."

"Five," said Grandma, "six next month. She won't get to start school until she's seven. It won't matter though, as small for her age as she is."

"Smart as a whip." The nurse reached in a cabinet, drew out bottles. "Bet she takes it after her grandmother."

Grandma laughed, patted Rilla's head.

Mama walked toward them, head down, blowing her nose.

"Stairs are this way." Grandma pushed toward the corner.

"Rilla and I will take the elevator." Mama watched the flashing numbers above the double doors.

"Stairs are quicker," Grandma said.

"I don't care." Mama blew her nose again.

"Suit yourself." Grandma snorted, banged shut the stair door.

"Five, four . . . here it comes." Rilla pranced.

Mama crumpled, recrumpled her tissues, tore them into small pieces.

In a concrete urn filled with sand and cigarette worms, Rilla buried her cap, covered it over like a cat. Nobody would ever find it and Grandma could not make her wear it now.

"Come on," Mama said as the elevator doors opened.

Rilla was pushed into a dark corner and the elevator started. It made her stomach hurt. She grabbed her mother's hand. "I want to get out. Let's go back."

Her mother laughed softly. "We can't go back."

Rilla couldn't breathe. Her chest hurt. "Let's go back."

"We're almost there," her mother whispered.

When the doors slid open, Rilla rushed into the lobby.

"We have to wait for Grandma," Mama said, looking up the stairs.

Rilla ran up, climbed a rail and locked herself around it. "I'm going to slide," she called to Mama below. "Catch me."

She flew and Mama caught her in a tangle of arms and legs, laughed, and hugged her close. "Mama," said Rilla, "I'm Daddy's girl, aren't I?"

"Yes," her mother said, "of course you are."

The Vinegar Jug

OVER COLD AND bitter coffee, Sharon said aloud thoughts she'd pushed around in her mind for a week. "You should have taken the job at the junior high."

"What?" Rob leaned around the sports section of the newspaper, stared at her. "Are you kidding? I couldn't handle it a month. That was no job, that was a sentence. Five days a week hard labor—breaking rocks. What makes you say I should've taken it?"

"Because"—she threw her spoon on the counter—"it would have been something."

"What?" He slapped the paper down. It slid off in a wide ruffle and drifted in a quiet flutter to the floor.

"A job." She gulped the last swallow of coffee, held the mug with both hands, tried to read the solemn stains on the bottom. "A job, that's what. J-O-B." She spelled the letters loud, distinct, final, sharp as broken glass.

"Is that all you think about? Like there's some magic to it?" He snapped his fingers, pinched the crisp air. "The answer to everything," he sneered.

"No, not everything, but part of it. Something."

He took his plate to the sink, stood with his back to her. He'd gained weight lately, thick around the middle. And he wasn't even good in bed any more. She hadn't said anything. Surely he knew.

"If that's what's worrying you," he said, "I'll get a job."

When? She wanted to say, but didn't. There was so much she didn't say lately.

"I'll dig ditches, if that's what . . . I'll . . ."

"Do it," she said quietly.

"What?" He stopped in the middle of the kitchen. He stood centered under the light fixture.

She got up and flicked it off. "Do it," she said. "Dig ditches, do something. I'm so tired of all this."

He stalked from the room, his face milk-white, blue eyes icy.

She put her face against the refrigerator, leaned on her arms, but didn't cry. It was too hot, too dry, she was too empty for it. She and the weather burned, parched, had no moisture. Only the woods around them had warning signs, no burning, no campfires, no smoking, watch your matches. She ought to have a sign like that to wear, too. One spark and she was off and roaring. She was disgusted with herself for yelling, for sounding exactly like the thing she had promised herself she never would be. A fishwife, a regular bitch. All the things she'd told herself she wouldn't ever say she'd said. And the ugly creature her words had made hopped around the empty room, made faces at her; green, purple, black Halloween witch faces.

In the beginning when Rob had been out of work two weeks, they joked about it. A vacation. It was great. What a life. Then a month, six months, now almost a year and they had stopped talking. Five days a week they had a pattern. There was a sort of tension, a hope. Businesses operated, schools were open, telephones rang; maybe theirs would. An answer to one of his ads, a letter, a contact he'd made would call. Saturdays were the end of hope. There was nothing to hide behind on Saturdays. No leads, as at first, little routes they traced zig, zag, zig on a map. Maps that went nowhere. He used to type resumés. She Xeroxed them at school. Impressive pages of credits, achievements, awards, publications.

"I'd hire you in a minute," she said once, hugged him as they looked over the pages he'd typed. Surely, somewhere there was a job for him, vacant, waiting and he would find it and fit in.

On the mornings she taught her class in Contemporary American Literature, he did the housework. Last year, they left together, going in opposite directions at the highway, honking and waving as they turned.

This year she went alone, left behind a mess in the bedroom, bath, kitchen. She never used to do that. She didn't like doing it now and she felt mean. It was a sort of rubbing it in. A reminder of who was important, who brought home the salary. Never mind how part-time it was, how small, never mind, only that it was *she* who brought it home. Home to the mess she left and he cleaned.

The first time she'd come home and found he'd cleaned the kitchen, she felt hurt and angry. She didn't know why. A puffy black anger that hung in the air like something burnt. And yet it was all she could do to keep from crying. Rob hated dishes! The kitchen work. He would do almost anything else in the house, vacuum, the bathrooms, scrub showers, floors, fixtures, wash, change beds—anything but dishes. Oh, he had done dishes several times, made a great show of washing and rinsing each piece, turning cup, bowl, plate carefully as a potter. Rinsing, wiping every tine of the forks, polishing pots, the stove. She tended to whisk through the kitchen, shove, stack, rattle, bang, but get the job done as quickly as possible, on to other things.

He followed her to the kitchen that first day like a child with a surprise on his face—a pleased look about his mouth. The kitchen sparkled, shone. Even the sink. He gestured like a salesman selling a house. "Look"—he pointed, rubbed his fingers across the hood of the stove—"no grease." He touched the top of the refrigerator. "No dust. It was thick as cloth up there. You never cleaned."

"I never looked up there," she said, and ducked into the hall. A laugh caught in her throat. She mumbled something about being in a hurry to go to the bathroom.

"You didn't say it was beautiful," he yelled.

"It's beautiful," she called behind her. "Marvelous, great, wonderful, terrific . . . how many adjectives do you need?"

After that, on her class morning, he cleaned and she never commented. Most of the time he had lunch out when she came home. Neat sandwiches, sliced tomatoes, soup, brownies on a plate. He was an adequate cook, but not good. She preferred hers, and cleaning the kitchen. What bothered her was knowing how much he hated doing dishes yet made himself do them, like a penance. Don't do this to yourself, she wanted to say, but didn't. There was so much she wanted to say and yet at times she felt she said too much. That she covered for him, protected him like an alcoholic's wife. Lying, but not quite, the times she told friends who asked, "Rob found a job?" She said he was working on his doctorate and had applied for a grant. That much was true. He had applied. And he had also been refused. To their friends she probably made it sound like he had the grant. The truth was that they were living on her salary from part-time teaching. Her meager two classes a week and promises for next year's full-time faculty. It was a small college, and they kept saying next year they would have a bigger budget, more funds; an endowment might come through. Rob had been the one with the secure job, a year to go to tenure. Her job was the iffy one, the fringe she was hanging onto reaching for the rope. Yet Rob's job had been the one canceled, his department discontinued, contract not renewed.

At first he'd had a few interviews, gone off whistling, excited. And he'd come back excited. "They seemed impressed with my qualifications." Then they never called back. The last interview had been in the middle of the year, a junior high two hundred miles away. They had called back, twice. "Biology," he said disgustedly. "They wanted me to teach biology and coach baseball."

She laughed. It was far from history, but there were books on the subject. And baseball. How much coaching was there to that?

"The pay," he said, "was ridiculous." He didn't have a certificate for public schools, only college.

They had talked about the job. Commuting was out of the question. She suggested he room over, come home weekends. Thoughts of being alone those nights frightened her. Could she manage? Make it on her own? If she had to.

Moving wasn't practical. The job was only for the rest of the school year and they could never find a place to live as cheaply as this. Their house was a cabin on the river and belonged to some friends of her parents who had chosen to travel for the winter. The Hoffmans also mentioned they might be interested in selling, since the cabin needed some repairs and was not in the most desirable section of the river lots anymore. What they had now, Sharon and Rob, was a sort of house-sitting arrangement. They paid utilities, and Rob was supposed to keep the heavy brush around the cabin trimmed, to make it look occupied, maybe prevent it from being burglarized. Last year, Sharon helped Rob clear brush, haul it to a ravine. All the while they watched for snakes. "Copperheads," Marvin Hoffman had told them. "They're around here. Color of leaves. You have to look for them." She and Rob had seen a few snakes, one on a rock by the river, a harmless water snake, another a black snake that she knew lived in the woodpile, also harmless.

Rob hated to clear brush, worried about snakes more than she did. "I wouldn't want to live out here with kids," he said once after they'd moved in.

Funny, and she had been the one holding back about having a child. Sharon wanted to wait until her teaching job was secure, when she would have maternity leaves, could schedule between semesters and all. Maybe security mattered more to her than to Rob. There were so many *ifs. If* Rob's tenure had come through, *if* Marvin Hoffman had sold them the cabin, *if* her job were permanent, *then* would be the time to have a baby. First things first, her mother always said. Order. Sharon like order and in the past Rob had been a big part of that order.

The cat, Smoky, a black Persian, rubbed against her leg and twined around her stool at the bar. Sharon sat back, let the cat leap into her lap, then stroked him until he settled down to a steady purr and kneading. She rubbed the cat's whiskers and noticed how gray he was getting.

"Thirteen's old for a cat," the vet said a few months ago. "Even a well-cared-for cat like this one."

Smoky had burned with fever, weak, had been no weight at all in her arms. "He may not make it through," Dr. Frazier had said.

The cat blinked green eyes, poked out a paw, washed.

She and Rob had taken turns getting the capsules, food, warm milk, and liquids into Smoky. Rob had been the one who set the clock for night medications. Several times she woke to lights on, Rob in the kitchen mixing medicine, heating milk. He would be like this with a child, she thought, a baby. A gentle, caring father.

"But it takes more than that," she told the cat who stopped washing and looked at her. "There's more to fathering than caring and 2:00 a.m. feedings, there's something called responsibility." The cat yawned wide and pink in her lap, its teeth shining thorns.

Their savings were almost gone. The savings they'd planned for a house, to travel, had melted like ice in August. Rob stopped writing resumes, reading ads. He worked off and on at a novel he had started the first year of their marriage. A book of dorm life, college pranks, panty raids, philosophical discussions. He hummed as he typed, distracted her as she corrected papers. He brought chapters for her to read, comment upon. She searched for things to say that wouldn't upset him, parts to praise. The truth was that academia had stilted his style, locked in his vocabulary. She tried to make suggestions for a clearer word, a description. He couldn't see them, argued, became loud.

The cat jumped off her lap, flicked his tail, and walked to the door. Sharon opened the door and heard a small, unusual noise. It took her a moment to decide the sound was Rob cutting brush. She saw his bare back in the woods, the flash of his axe. She hadn't heard him get his tools, hadn't heard the door of the workshop.

Sharon stacked plates, ran water, filled the sink with a great crest of suds. She watched Rob bend as he worked. Work. He was willing to switch jobs with her without hesitation. She'd helped him cut brush before. It wasn't the worst job in the world. Not the most pleasurable, but not the worst. No worse than scrubbing a burned black pot of greasy stew. Cutting brush was at least outdoors and had compensations. Number one, it was not an everyday thing. Number two, you had a sense of accomplishment when you finished. Number three, you never knew what you'd find. She'd found some unusual wildflowers . . . a carnivorous plant, she remembered; a blue-tailed skink; and once, the most beautiful blue beetle. The real thing, she told herself, was not jobs, nor roles, nor attitudes . . . maybe it was attitudes. What it boiled down to—she rinsed a spoon—was that she didn't want a wife for a husband. She didn't want someone who cleaned and cooked. Who kissed her goodbye at the door and drank coffee all day. (It could be worse, she told herself in a faraway-her-mother's-kind-of-voice.) Sure it could, in all kinds of ways, but, Sharon told herself, what she really wanted was a husband, someone to share, take on half at least. She dried a glass, put it in a row with others on the shelf. Her feelings, spread out, looked to be of various sizes and though not as clear as the glasses, at least recognizable.

Rob's axe flashed in the sunlight as he swung. She wiped the counter, glanced out the window, and saw he had stopped and was standing, staring at the ground. Had he hurt himself? He was good with tools, careful, and though he didn't use them regularly, kept them oiled, dry, and in good repair.

"Rob," she called, "what is it?"

The McClintocks' dogs, a collie named Dan and a part-shepherd, Lady, pawed the ground, whined, barked, their tails in the air like a workman swinging warning flags. "Get away," he yelled to the dogs. "Stay back."

Sharon almost tripped on the loose bottom step of the deck as she ran.

"Don't come up here," Rob called. "Stay back."

"What happened?" She still held the damp dish towel, walking closer.

"A copperhead." He leaned on his axe, almost smiling. "I think I killed him, but I want to be sure." His voice had more excitement in it than she'd heard in weeks.

"Where?" She was beside him now, looking into the brush, curled leaves.

"By the stump," he pointed.

She saw the twisted white underneath of the snake and shuddered, wrapping her arms tight about herself.

"I almost didn't see it." Rob poked leaves with a rake. "It moved when the dogs came up or I would have stepped on it."

He lifted the snake on the end of the rake, the metal fingers waving it like a string. "About a foot long, wouldn't you say?"

The snake looked small to her . . . and large. Limp, dangling, dead, but with a large frightening danger about it.

Rob flung the dead snake into the woods, where it caught on the lower limb of a beech tree and swung. They watched it swing like a warning. He could have been bitten. God, it was close. And she was the one who screamed, Get a job, dig ditches, do something, anything, I don't care. And he had. He'd killed a snake. A thing he feared for the two years they had been here. She shivered. What if he had been killed? It would have been her fault. No, damn it, not her fault. She started crying, shaking from her shoulders down, her eyes burning.

She walked to him, slid her hand around his waist, dipped slightly inside his pants to the small of his back. His flesh was cool, hard there beneath the denim. "I'm sorry," she said.

He twisted away, threw the rake like a spear into the woods. "I hope you're satisfied now."

The rake hit a tree like a hand, clattered to the ground, hits metal fingers frantic and ringing in the still woods.

"You said do something. 'Dig ditches.'" He mimicked her voice. "I could have been killed, thanks to you. Clear your own damn woods." He stalked to the deck, stopped once to wipe his forehead.

"It's not my fault," she started, then stopped. His axe lay beside the rotten stump where the snake had been. She picked it up, swung a blow to the stump which shattered into a brown powder that steamed in the air like a smoldering volcano. She kicked the stump, stepped on it hard, tamped it flat with the ground. What if there were more snakes? A teeming mass of them. She didn't care. Let them come. She'd destroy the copperhead castle.

Beside the stump had been a patch of the moss she used in terrariums. Gardens she made for friends, gifts she sent with a note when the occasion demanded—"A little bit of me under glass"—to cheer the sick, to celebrate the new baby, the promotion. She used to give books. She loved to give books and delighted in taking a long time in their choosing, the right one for the right person and special event. She took joy in their wrapping. Books made their own boxes, which was more than she could say for terrariums. She collected various containers, sizes, shapes and at one point, made them for the local florist. Rob had added up her costs, said she was only kidding herself that she was making any money, so she had stopped. Whatever it was she supposedly hadn't made had helped buy more at the grocery store, she remembered, and he hadn't complained about that.

Sharon cut and stacked brush. At one point she cut down a good-sized dogwood that hadn't bloomed this spring. It was hollow and black in the center around the pink heart. She sawed it into logs, pushing, pulling the curve-handled hand saw across the tree until it lay sectioned. Her wrists ached and there was a blister on her thumb.

She didn't think of snakes anymore. Or anyone. Or anything. Only the cutting, sawing, clearing of the area around her. Gnats buzzed around her at times, and she brushed them away along with the sweat from her face and neck. She was surprised once when some perspiration ran into her eyes and burned. It actually stung for a moment.

She picked up the logs and carried them to the stack beside the door.

The cat sat washing himself on the steps. He turned one wise eye toward her like a wink. She rolled the wood from her arms with a clatter, straightened it and noticed there was enough for several weeks of heating. If it ever turned cold. She couldn't remember what cold was like, only that it seemed clean to her and like something desirable.

She stopped to stroke the cat, who arched under her hand, rubbed against her leg. The hand that fed him and all that clichéd stuff, she thought. When he wasn't hungry, he was Rob's cat and wouldn't have anything to do with her. At times he hissed when she walked past his chair. Rob would laugh.

The stack of brush she had piled looked like a thatched hut from here, or an airy mountain. She'd like to light a match to it, finish the job. The air itself hung so hot, she felt it would spark, that one snap of her fingers and a blaze would flash, the green limbs crackle, burn orange coals, and become a mound of sifted gray ashes. She didn't know if the brush would ever get burnt. Rob tended to walk away from the things, not go back and finish. Actually the brush decayed and as it did, it made a protective thicket for birds and other wildlife.

The snake still hung on the limb, black, like a deep gash

or wound against the tree trunk. She would have thrown that in the blaze, like a symbol, a gift, an offering to some god. She didn't know which one. The God of Eve? She snickered at the irony of her own thinking, her joke.

Sharon wiped her feet on the mat, noticing it was worn almost beyond the point of being effective. She heard the roar of a football game: "First down and twenty. The Black Hawks really want to win this one, folks." Rob's chair squeaked as she walked past and into the kitchen. He held a can of the coldest-looking beer. Frost driblets down the sides made her tongue wet.

She saw he'd left the bread open from his lunch, the small blue plastic twistem beside the sprawling loaf. There was a blob of wasted grape jelly on the knife and the lid was off the peanut butter.

She opened the refrigerator, rummaged behind the orange juice, milk, and container of tea, then checked the back of the bottom shelf, atop the meat-keeper, where they sometimes kept beer to get really cold. In the back corner, behind a jar of olives, she felt a can and pulled it out, tasting it already. Then she blinked when she saw the colors of the can. Refrigerator Deodorizer. She turned it around in her hand, half-laughing, half-crying. Then she read the expiration date—June . . . of last year. Last year.

In a haze she spun around, hit jars and bottles on the refrigerator shelf, knocked over a jar of dill pickles. It teetered, turned over as she grabbed at it, and spilled a yellow brine down the shelf, which dripped into a puddle on the floor.

"The Vinegar Jug," she thought. "An old man and an old woman lived in a vinegar jug . . ." Two pickles leaned on the dry side of the jar.

In the bedroom, she got her car keys, purse, counted twelve dollars, plus the checkbook with almost a hundred in it, her overnight case with pajamas, robe, slippers, bra, and panties. Last, she folded in a shirtwaist dress and belt her mother had sent last year for her birthday and some dress sandals. She pushed the lid tight, grabbed the handle, and walked out. Rob didn't glance up from the game. An announcer blared, "And the Hawks are behind by seven—this may be the winning play."

All the way down the drive, she composed letters. Dear Dr. Ornsby, Due to unforeseen circumstances . . . Dear Marvin and Frances, Thank you for the use of the cabin . . .

When she thought of him finding the puddle of brine, she laughed. She hoped he'd think it was urine.

The Summer Kitchen

MARIE IS MAKING jelly. Wild-grape jelly. The whole kitchen smells wonderfully ripe-purple. Even the steam above the stove is mauve and singing. Marie hums, alone and into the night, where the kitchen of this summer cabin is probably the only light for miles. She wears one of her husband's old shirts knotted at her waist, and panties. Her feet are bare. She likes to be barefoot on the cool kitchen floor late at night. And she likes a kitchen when nothing is expected of her, when no one will interrupt.

Earlier she pinned her blonde hair back, and then finally up and off her neck. That helped cool her in the steamy kitchen that slowly cools now in the fuzzy black night.

Three cats sit outside on the windowsill, watching her work. Marie likes to cook for an audience, even if the audience is only cats. The cats yawn one, three, two, as if she pointed a baton at them. Shame on you, she tells herself, keeping cats up past their bedtime. Through the screen, the cats stare; green eyes large as owls' follow Marie as she moves from sink to cabinet to stove, opening drawers, measuring sugar. She doesn't want to add sugar at all, the grape juice is so pure and strong. She wishes it were strong enough to stand, jell of its own strength. She feels she is cheating to add pectin to it, change it, charge it to become a product, bottled and practical, but that is all she knows to do at the moment. The only guide she has came with pectin the bottle.

The grape juice has dyed everything it touched. Dishtowels, wooden spoon halfway up its handle, cups, bowls, counter, sink, Marie's fingers, a spot on her shirt. Jon's old shirt. She thinks the spot won't come out quickly, maybe never, and will go through washings to remind her. She'll wear it like a badge. Perhaps add others it to like colors on an artist's smock, her uniform of the jellymaker's trade. And Jon will find it funny, his old shirt gone soft next to her skin, hugging her breasts.

If Jon were home now, he'd be reading. She wonders how many tax accountants read Emerson. Thoreau. Emily Dickinson. He often reads aloud to her in the kitchen, sentences, paragraphs, prefacing them with an excited "Listen to this . . ." She misses his presence, his voice. At first, these summers, they telephoned each other a lot. Late at night. But he would be tired and she would be reading, or sleepy. What they said were not the things they wanted to say. Now they each save moments for the weekends. Lovely things they share like small, specially wrapped packages. Or collected coins, polished and dated, labeled.

If her sons were up, they would be playing checkers or a marble and dice game. They would not check to see what she cooked because it was not near a mealtime. If they saw the juice, they would not taste it as Marie did, tasting it in the morning by the lake, sun and dew and air heavy with wine. Marie is making jelly because she does not know how to make wine. Oh, what wonderful wine her father made in their damp and moldy dark cellar. She does not have kegs and crocks, white cloths to strain it through, thermometers. She remembers the more-than-grape smell, the heavy Burgundy air.

Marie has used a worn pillowcase for a jelly bag. She hung it above the blue-enamel cooking pot like an udder, warm and soft, squeezed it ever so gently, against the directions that cautioned not. She had listened to the drip of it all afternoon, through supper. They ate on the stone back steps and it comforted her to know the bag dripped without her there to order it, direct it. The jelly juice still dripped as she bathed the boys, let them run squealing and naked to thin pajamas and bunkbeds. It seems ages ago that she checked their curled and dream-wrapped sleep, before her pot of purple broth simmered and talked.

Marie stirs and wishes she knew words or chants to make her jelly magic, full of health and vitamins and summer. But she does not know chants or charms, so she hums and stirs, does small dance steps with her old woodstove partner. "Home Comfort." She loves the name, the ornate bowed legs, the little oven and warming cupboards above. She found the stove at an auction and Jon sanded, polished, and blacked until it gleamed like a genie's lamp.

She wishes Jon were here. That he could be a part of the kitchen late at night, enveloped, both of them, in the winy air. Breathing purple, watching everything through shades of lavender and pink. It seems Jon is never there when special things, little things, happen, and their magic is lost when she tells him. She can never quite capture that moment again in talk or telling.

He was in the city the night owls held a summer convention in their trees. Owls called and winged great, heroic speeches, nominations, orations across the lake. Marie and the boys, awake and sleepily subdued in the silver light of 3:00 a.m., watched from the porch. "I didn't know owls could be so big," Jess said when they told Jon about it that weekend.

"So loud!" Martin made a face. "They scared me."

"Not my brave Indian." Jon ruffled Martin's thick red curls.

"Not really," Martin said. "Not next time."

"They were mating," Jon said later.

"Nine owls?" Marie asked. "It was the Southern Owl Association Big Meeting and Annual Convention. I know political speeches when I hear them. Nominations and seconds. Great horned hooting."

He rubbed the back of her neck. "How about pre-mating?"

"I accept that." She laughed. "Owl expert."

Actually he was the hawk watcher, keeping a tally each week of ones he saw beside the interstate. They seemed to like the clear vistas and high wires over the backwoods for hunting. He'd become quite a spotter, and one week reported he'd seen a hawk perched atop the steeple of a small white church on a hill above the highway. He had borrowed her worn leather bird book until she bought him one of his own. The last time she looked, he was still in the hawks section.

Marie was the only one to see the herd of deer move silently through their back yard. Does, thirty-five to fifty of them, and not an antler among the pack. They were the color of tree trunks as they weaved through the woods. She wasn't really sure she was seeing them until they were gone. But afterward their hoofprints patterned the creek banks, and she had those to show the boys and Jon. Heart-shaped prints embossed in the red clay. They were there for weeks. She wondered if the deer had even stopped for water or had simply, silently, continued their journey.

Jon was also away the afternoon shortly after she saw the does, when she heard a barrage of shots in the woods. The boys were on the porch, but she was apprehensive, thinking of the deer herd. Were they being chased by hunters? She called the game warden, who came in his brown car. Later he pulled into the drive and leaned out to tell her the hunters weren't hunters after game but were shooting swags of mistletoe from the tops of a stand of oaks. Nothing illegal.

When the road and creek and drive flooded, Jon missed it. For a week the creek roared like something gone wild. And she thought the rain would never stop. The boys, after exhausting every board game and puzzle in the place, resorted to building forts with the sofa cushions and pelting each other with jellybeans. On Friday, the first day of sun, the creek's waters pooled and spread like an ocean. They watched, fascinated, most of the day while water covered the drive, yard and bridge and swallowed a gap of road. They weren't afraid. The house was high above the creek, out of the way and dry. But all of them worried that Jon would get stranded on the other side. Would he park the car and walk? If he walked, where would he cross? Swim, with his clothes and briefcase? But the waters receded even faster than they came, left twigs and sticks in a dark ring where they had been. Jon examined the residue with them—wet logs and beaver "jam-up" (the boys called it) where the creek narrowed. For weeks afterward they talked of "When the creek flooded" and "Remember when the creek came way up here?"

Jess and Martin were the ones to find wild grapes. They'd come in with tongues and fingers stained.

"There's lots and lots," Martin said, pulling her to come see.

Lots and lots usually meant a handful. Summers before, Marie had left the few scattered grapes she saw for the birds and foxes. But she let the boys lead her to vines near the lake, near where the tree house stood. The lake where Jon taught Jess and Martin to swim last summer. Every Sunday morning, until the water was too, too cold, she watched them from her seat in the pines. Watched their bodies arch and dive, shiny as fish. Liking earth more than water, Marie brought along her bird book and binoculars, or her cross-stitch with its crayon-box colors of threads.

To her surprise, there were a lot of grapes. The air was ripe, alive with their wine smell. The vines hung heavy with sleek purple marbles. She ate one, then another, and more, let the wild juice linger as she chewed the tart, thick hulls. They were wonderful and she had to do something with them. To keep them. Make use of them.

All was quiet except for the *plop* as she piled grapes in her basket, the soft *swish* of leaves as she pulled them close, picked, let go, her fingers fuzzy. She felt steeped in grape smell and so heady she could have been drunk as she walked back to the cabin.

Drunk on the sweet, wild smell. A smell thick enough to spoon over ice cream or drink from the air. That world of grapes that must have been before people, before animals, before God? Maybe at one time there were only God and grapes and the air was wine.

Marie ladles foam off the simmering jelly into a saucer. Lavender whipped cream. A test as old as time. She remembers her grandmother, here in the kitchen, letting Marie taste the warm jelly, the lace around it.

She takes the jars from their boiling bath, sets them on a clean, spread dishtowel, pours jelly. Five full jars of jelly. She doesn't spill a drop as the dark-purple waterfall goes into glasses that have been waiting for this all their lives.

Her pot is empty except for a wedge of juice in the bottom. Not even half a glass. What to do? She pours it into a custard cup, where it sits like a small purple pudding.

Then she puts lids on hot jars, holds each one tight with a towel and twists, amazed at her own strength, sureness. She sets the jars aside in a row as orderly as a church pew. She sighs and stares around her. The kitchen is purple. Purple as the night outside. She looks and even the cats have gone to bed. Marie would like to leave right now, tiptoe out, flip off the light, and fall into bed. But she can't. She knows everything will be sticky in the morning. Pans, spoons, colander, counter. The floor is gritty, grained with sugar and sand.

She fills the sink with hot water and suds, begins. Not humming now, but working with speed and determination to rinse, dry, put away. Wiping stove and sink until at last everything is clean. The smell of grapes lingers and she takes the pulp, gray as eggplant, to the porch. Tomorrow she will spread it in the woods, return a share to the soil, the bees.

She gives the jars one more loving look, holds one up to

the light. It is like looking through stained glass. She reverently sets the jar down. Its sister jar pings. Then another. Seals of approval. Comforting chimes of a distant clock.

Marie thinks of Jon, asleep in their house in the city. Three hours away. Alone. And she is alone. She wishes there were a way she could slip out of herself and into his bed until morning. Then back to motherhood, to self, to here. She sighs, takes one last look around the clean kitchen in the bare white light, sees the lonely custard cup of jelly. She takes a spoon from the drawer, holds the jelly high and spoons up the still-warm liquid, savoring each special drop. Then she turns out the light.

The Swing

THE ROOM SMELLED of old hymn books, dust, and stale dry air. One window was curtained by two lengths of dark green plastic that once hung in someone's home.

When amid the opening, closing, and rustling of purses, the wooden collection plate of the Mary Magdelene Sunday School Class was passed to Margaret Rivers, she held it in her hands a moment, then passed it to Ellie Mason. Ellie Mason sniffed once, laid her dollar bill on the others, snapped her big black purse shut with a loud click, and passed the plate down the row.

Margaret could hear the low buzz of women's voices follow the collection plate around the room. Like hornets abuilding a nest, she thought. Let them talk, I don't care. She pulled a handkerchief from the loose bosom of her blue dotted-swiss dress, spread it across her knees, and began to smooth the folds. With the tip of her index finger she traced the bumps of the spray of forget-me-nots embroidered in one corner. These don't look like my hands, she thought suddenly. They look so rough and red, like I just took them out of the washtubs. She turned the strange hands over in her lap. Papa always said I had such small hands. She sighed, quickly refolded the handkerchief, placed it in the middle of the black Bible in her lap, and glanced at the pink and purple map of the Holy Land that hung on the wall behind the teacher's desk.

"Mrs. Rivers." Letitia Hinson spoke from behind the desk. "I thought I'd call on our preacher's wife to lead us in our opening prayers this morning."

The sharp voice rapped out the command and Margaret was trapped by the dozen now silent and tight-lipped women. She shut her eyes, bowed her head, and began.

"Our Father"—yes, that was right, she was glad she remembered. "Our Father," she repeated. Father was Papa who never said a cross word to her in his life. "Thank you for every blessing we have received." Papa was so good to her. She was breathing more evenly now. "Bless us during the lesson this morning and be with us during the coming week. Amen." She finished, raised her head, and swallowed the lump that had grown to her throat.

Margaret did not hear the Sunday School lesson. It droned on and on like the constant irritation of a distant sawmill. She dutifully opened her Bible to the appropriate scriptures and sat watching the black letters run together like watery ink. When she heard the thud of Bibles being closed, she hastily shut hers too and stood in front of her chair while Letitia's long benediction rained like dust particles on her head.

When it was over, she reached up, felt for a wisp of hair and tucked it back into the tight, round onion of a bun on the back of her neck. I'm the only woman in the class not wearing a hat, she thought as she looked around the milling group. That should give their tongues something else to wag about next week, and she walked out.

Behind her, she could hear the chant. Nice lesson, Letitia; enjoyed the lesson, Letitia; a real blessing, Letitia. Bunch of hypocrites. She slammed the door. The hall was crowded and she weaved past groups of smiling, talking people who smelled faintly of fried pork, Rose hair oil and vanilla flavoring.

Just as she curled her fingers around the cold doorknob, he grasped her shoulder. She could feel the pressure of every finger.

His voice was a hoarse whisper, angry as wind. "Stay for the service, Margaret. It won't kill you."

She spun around. "What for? To hear you make a fool of yourself?"

He flushed dark and it spread to the inlets of his almost bald head, tinting his sparse white hair a pale pink. His mouth jerked open slightly as though he wanted to say more, but dared not.

Margaret yanked the doorknob, stepped outside and pulled the door shut with glass-rattling force, then leaned against the side of the building; rough edges of peeling paint picking through the thinness of her dress. A small breeze lifted her collar; she turned her face to catch the air and saw the cemetery, fenced with blackberry briars. High as my head, she thought, and nobody gives a hoot. Ellie Mason and them just laugh about all the pies they've had from cemetery vines. Her eyes followed the weed-tufted gravel path to the center of the cemetery and the largest stone. She knew the inscription by heart: "Lilly Reiley Rivers, Beloved Wife of Daniel Polkton Rivers, Her Price Is Far Above Rubies." Had to buy her the fanciest stone in the cemetery, lilies carved on it till there's not a place you can lay your finger. And my babies; my babies was lucky to get a marker.

The door behind Margaret opened, and children ran past like a herd of freed ponies; slick-haired boys yelled and whooped; little girls in bell-shaped dresses, their heads bent together in giggles, brushed past. Not one of them Laura. Margaret leaned back to wait. From the front of the church she could hear the squeak, squawk of the pump, the clang of the tin cup, and squeals at the rush of water.

The door opened scarcely larger than a crack and Laura

squeezed out, head bent like an old lady.

Margaret laughed. "Cow's tail. You're always the last one out." As soon as the words were spoken she wanted them back. Laura's small face was pinched, her eyes large and wet under the severe line of dark bangs. She's tenderhearted like me, Margaret thought, not one to take teasing. "What's wrong, honey?" she asked gently.

Laura twisted a small handkerchief with both hands. "I couldn't get the knot loose, Maw Maw. I tried and tried and it wouldn't come undone."

Margaret took the crumpled handkerchief and began to pull at the knotted lump. "Honey, you got it wet, that's why. You worried with it so much you made it tighter." She tucked the Bible under her arm and began to pick at the knot. "Hold your hands under here and catch the pennies when I get 'em loose or they'll fly all over creation."

Laura cupped her hands under Margaret's large ones and when the pennies dropped, she caught them. "What'll I do with them now?" She pointed with her chin toward the doorway. "Take them in there?"

"Pshaw, I'd not bother." Margaret clasped her lips together in a tight line. "Just keep 'em yourself."

"I don't care what HE says." Margaret began to walk quickly around the church and through the yard. Laura ran to keep up. Behind them church doors closed with a loud scrape.

"Brin-ging in the sheaves, brin-ging in the sheaves." The voices rolled over their heads and Miss Bessie at the piano tinkled in the extra notes she was known for. "Weee shall come rejoicing, brin-ging in the sheaves."

Margaret muttered, "Picked out the songs too, didn't he?"

"How do you know?" Laura asked, and stopped to grab a fallen oak limb.

They walked toward the old baptismal house, its paint gone, the weathered boards a greenish tint of moss growing between the cracks. Its tin roof was the color of red clay and two doors, side by side, faced steps that led down to the dirt-crusted concrete pool.

Laura ran down the steps and began to lift pieces of wet, yellow paper and leaves with her stick. "Look, Maw Maw, somebody's old shoe's in here." She kicked it.

"Better get out of there before you get snakebit." Margaret said to Laura's dark head bobbing on the steps. She looks so much like Mary; little spindly legs, I worried they'd not make it up those steps. She was twelve and not much bigger than Laura. I tried to tell him that Sunday she was sick. He just felt her forehead, said it didn't feel hot, so get ready. I begged him to let her stay in bed. He said I was always putting my children before the Lord and I'd be punished for it. It was punishing that child to make her go.

"Margaret," Laura yelled from the third step, "was my daddy baptized here? Did they put him all the way under?"

"All of 'em were. All four of my children that lived were baptized here . . . and it like to have killed Mary. All week she hadn't been pert and I'd seen the stain on her britches. Knew it was coming on her. Dreaded it. Saturday night she was bent double with cramps. I filled the hot water bottle, wrapped it in an old sheet. Only thing I knew to ease it. The rest you got to live with, I told her. It ain't easy being a woman."

"Did she almost drown?" Laura was beside her now, skipping in the path across the broomstraw field.

"Who? Did who almost drown?"

"Aunt Mary?"

The saliva was bitter in Margaret's mouth. "No, it wasn't that atall. Something you wouldn't understand." The water in that pool was like ice, coming from the spring like it did, and Palm Sunday in March. I worried, was cold all over for her. He put her under and she came up dripping, face white as the dress she had on. When I heard a scream from the dressing-room after they had gone back, I tore in there. Scared me weak to my knees to see her laying on the floor, limp as a rag. I got somebody to take us home; left him standing in the water still preaching. He didn't speak to me that day, kept his jaws shut tighter than a bear trap. Mary took pneumonia after that and like to have died—he's made a fool of himself more than once in that church.

Laura stood at the edge of the woods under a large tree. "Let's pick up hickory nuts, Maw Maw."

"It's too early." Margaret gave a short laugh. "They ain't fell yet. Wait till the leaves turn; you come back and stay with Maw Maw then and we'll pick up hickory nuts."

Laura hit the tree trunk with her stick. "I bet we get a bushel."

"Don't count on it." Margaret pointed to the top of the tree. "See those dead limbs. This tree's old. Your daddy and us picked many a bushel of hickory nuts, took 'em up town and sold 'em. Most we ever got was fifty cents a bushel. Course that was big money in those days."

"I'll get a dollar for mine." Laura jumped flat-footed over a big root.

"Whoa now, missy." Margaret's voice was tinged with amusement. "You're talking mighty big for such a little girl."

"Well," Laura said, her lips in a pout, "I'm getting that five-dollar gold piece, aren't I?"

"Don't count your chickens till they hatch, I've always said." Margaret walked ahead, leaned over and broke off a handful of pine needles, bent them across her hand and lifted them to her nose. Pine smelled so clean. He don't turn loose much for his family. Church now, that's different. It's in the name of the Lord.

They entered a thick grove of pines. Laura threw away her stick and walked sliding her feet under pine needles like two small plows.

"This is where your daddy wanted to build a house," Margaret said, and Laura didn't answer. There was only the soft shuffling in the dry needles. "HE wouldn't have it though, said selling this lot would cut up the farm. Lot's already off from the rest of the land and it will never be any good unless the church wants it. Church don't need it."

Margaret snorted. "Just his excuse."

Through the trees Margaret could see the black stretch of road, and across from that the rusted mailbox leaned on its rotten post. On top of the hill she could see the squat, reddish house, roof so bright it hurt her eyes. Painted it silver so folks'd think we had a new one. And that siding. Made to look like brick, but ain't. Any fool would know the difference. I wanted the house painted white if he was going to have anything done after all these years. My daddy always had our house painted white. Outbuildings too. Everybody always said we had the prettiest farm.

"Take holt my hand, Laura." Margaret shaded her eyes. "Guess we'd hear a car if one was coming." She checked both ways before they walked across.

Laura stood on tiptoes, pulled the mailbox lid, and peeped into the warm blackness. "It's empty."

Margaret stretched over her. "Let me see. Mail don't run on Sunday, but we might find something we missed yesterday." She patted the bottom of the box, ran her fingers around the corner, and thumped the back before shutting the lid with a dull clang. "One time a letter from Paul got stuck in the back and I didn't find it for over a week. I worried something terrible. I always get a letter from him on Mondays, 'less the mail don't run."

They started down the unpaved road, Margaret in one rut, Laura in the other, tall grass between.

Laura counted on her fingers, "You get a letter from Uncle Paul on Mondays, the *Saturday Evening Post* on Tuesdays, a letter from Aunt Mary on Wednesdays—what do you get the rest of the week, Maw Maw?"

Margaret laughed. "Not much! You got my mail all figured out, haven't you?"

Laura shook her head. The pigtails swung like twin whips. "Huh uh. I can't figure out why you get the *Saturday Evening Post* on Tuesdays. If they call it the *Saturday Evening Post* you ought to get it on Saturdays."

"Some folks get theirs on Saturday, I 'spect. I'm lucky to

get mine on Tuesdays, whatever they want to call it. I don't complain."

They had begun to climb the hill now. On each side of the road, remains of the old orchard stood, trees gnarled like lepers' limbs.

"No siree." Margaret's breath was shallow and fast. "I don't complain as long as I get it." And Paul said he'd see to it I got the *Saturday Evening Post* the rest of my life if I wanted it . . . and after his daddy wrote and told him not to send that trash. 'Course I wrote in the same mail and said don't do no sucha thing. He keeps wondering when the subscription's out. Nothing fit to read but the Bible, HE's said time and time again. And every Sunday morning he starts the kitchen fire with my magazine. Rips it up page by page. I used to put my hands over my ears so I wouldn't have to hear it. Now I just go about my business and pay it no mind. I get a brand new copy on Tuesday and HE can't stand it. "Laura," she said suddenly, with more sharpness than she intended, "quit thinking about the *Saturday Evening Post* and let's work on your memorizing."

"I said my verses good yesterday, didn't I?"

"Yes, but that was yesterday and if you stumble one time he won't give you the five-dollar gold piece," Margaret said to the back of Laura's head. "He won't tell you the next word either."

"I know what," Laura looked back with a sideways grin, her eyes bright as a kitten's. "I'll study while you fix dinner. Listen to me say the first part now." Laura brushed her bangs to one side and began to sing-song, "The Lord is my shepherd, I shall not want. He maketh me to lie down in green pastures, he . . ."

Margaret paced each step with the words and when they reached the top of the hill said, "Slow down, honey, let me catch my breath." She took several deep breaths. "I was getting kinda swimmy-headed."

Across the front of the house on the open porch, wooden chairs leaned, their rockers upended like a row of menacing horns. At the far end a swing moved slightly in the breeze.

"Let's swing, Maw Maw." Laura's heels clicked like small horse hooves across the porch.

"We better fix dinner," Margaret said. "Your daddy and mama might come and he'll be home shortly after twelve unless he gets wound up and forgets to stop." She chuckled.

"Just for a minute?" Laura patted the empty space beside her.

Margaret grasped the cedar post, pulled herself up on the porch, and plopped down beside Laura. "It does feel good." She leaned back. "I always did like a swing. We had one at home."

"Just like this?"

"No, it was wicker, white wicker with green cushions in it and many a night Dora, Elsie, or Pearl did their courting in it."

"Did you, Maw Maw?"

"No, I never did," Margaret's face was solemn. "I never courted atall. 'Thirty-five years old and not married. Who'll look after you when I'm gone,' Papa said. 'You don't want to be a burden on your sisters and their families. Preacher Rivers is a good man, Margaret. He needs another wife. A good man!'" Margaret spit out a piece of grit that was cutting her tongue. "God Himself that's who he thinks he is. Me and my children laboring on this farm, him off in his white shirt preaching. And when they wanted some little something he'd say it was sinful. I bought this swing," she said to Laura. "I bought and paid for it with my own money when your daddy wasn't any bigger than you are now. Paul and Mary saw this swing in Kistler's hardware store and commenced begging for it. Red, it was bright red then, bright as a Christmas bow. Sinful to spend money on foolishness, he said, work of the Devil. I'd not seen those kids want anything as bad as that swing in a long time. I went to the bank and drew out seven dollars of the money Papa left me and bought it. He was so mad he was about to pop, rared and pitched all the way home; kids huddled together in the back seat like they had been whipped. Me and the kids put it up that night while he was at prayer meeting. He's never sat in it to this day, acts like it's not even here. I've seen him bump into it many a time." Margaret smiled a thin halfmoon and ran her fingers along the wooden arm. "Hasn't been painted since David was home from service that summer, 'fore he was killed. He put in new boards, sanded it, and kept teasing about how pretty the blue swing was going to look. Had me worried for a while, till he called me to come see it when he finished. It was red, shiny as new." Margaret rubbed the dead paint into a powder between her fingers. "Needs painting again now."

Laura stood up and brushed off the back of her dress. "It sure does."

"Good heavens," Margaret said suddenly and stood. "I hear cars leaving from the church. Must be twelve and we got to get some dinner on the table. Let's make haste."

Laura held the door for her grandmother and they walked quickly down the narrow hall, past the front room with its black leather chairs and grass rug and the front bedroom where Laura and her grandmother had slept this week.

In the kitchen, Margaret grabbed her feed sack apron from its nail and slid it over her head, tying it deftly at the waist. She poked the fire and noticed a few shiny staples, some irregular bits of paper. She picked up a brown-edged triangle, turned it over, and said, "Tugboat Annie," then crumpled it and tossed it back in the stove.

Laura came into the kitchen as Margaret opened a mildew-covered jar of dark purple. "Damson," Margaret said. "Taste them." She gave Laura a spoon, then emptied the preserves onto the yellow circle of cake. "Not much, but it'll give plain cake a little flavor." Margaret licked the knife, then set the cake in the middle of the oilcloth-covered table. "Say your verses for me, honey, real quick."

Laura leaned over the back of the chair. "Make a joyful noise unto the Lord, all ye lands. Serve the Lord with gladness . . ."

Margaret looked at the page in the Bible on the table. "Come before his presence . . ." She took spoons and forks from a glass on the table and laid three places.

At the sound of a car, Laura lifted the corner of a muslin curtain. "Somebody in a blue car brought Granddaddy home."

Margaret poured water into a skillet, laid biscuits left from breakfast onto a plate, clanged the lid, and set it on the stove. "Brother Bassett, I 'spect." She stood in the doorway and watched as he put his notebook and the big zippered Bible on the small table by the window. "Dinner's ready, but I thought we'd wait and see if Dan and Julie come first."

He took off his black coat and hung it inside the closet on a nail. Slightly stooped, but lean and tall, he radiated strength. Don't look any more seventy than he did forty when we got married, Margaret thought.

He patted Laura on the head. "How's my girl?" Then turned to Margaret and said matter-of-factly, "I'm not eating cold."

Margaret checked the biscuits just starting to steam, stirred the pot of beans, and put chicken dumplings in a bowl. "Wonder what's keeping your daddy and mama?" she said to Laura and hugged her close. "Guess they ain't coming and I'll have to keep you." She cupped her hands on each side of Laura's face. "You could live with Maw Maw all the time then."

"And not go to school?" Laura's eyes were wide. She pulled away. "I've got to go to school."

"I know you have, honey." Margaret brushed one of Laura's pigtails back. "I was just teasing. Maw Maw wants you to go to school and learn everything you can so you'll grow up to be independent. Support yourself. Not have to depend on somebody else."

He stood at the table, white shirt open, exposing a neck wrinkled and scrawny as an old turkey's wattle. "What's holding up dinner?" He pulled out a chair. "I've got to be at a meeting at Shiloh at two." He poured a glass of buttermilk.

"I may preach their revival again this year." He folded his hands in his lap.

Margaret put the hot biscuits on a plate, covered them with a cloth, set them on the table, and took her place. Laura sat with her palms together under her chin.

"Bless this food, Our Father," he said, and Margaret bowed her head. "To the use of our bodies. And bless . . ."

Margaret's stomach tightened, rolled, then murmured as he went on and on. "Bless the Worseley family," he was saying. "Thou has seen fit to take their youngest from them."

Yes, Margaret thought, and he's better off than in that squalor.

"We knowest not why, Our Father, but we must trust in Thy divine plan. Bless . . ." His voice was like an old motor grinding, yet running forever.

Finally Margaret coughed, cracked an eyelid at Laura, who seemed to be asleep. Poor thing, his Sunday blessings are enough to last us a week.

"Amen," he said flatly, raised his head, took a sip of buttermilk and reached for a biscuit. "Cold." He laid it on his plate. "Biscuit's no good if it won't melt butter." He picked up his fork and raked chicken dumplings onto his plate.

Margaret pressed her lips together and reached for the salt shaker.

"Today's the day, Missy." He shoved a bite of chicken into his mouth. "You going to say your verses for me?"

"After lunch." Margaret took a swallow of coffee, "let her eat."

When he had cleaned his plate he reached for the cake, plunged a knife in its center, and pushed down until the plate rocked. "Wrap up what's left of this, Margaret." He lifted a piece of cake on his plate, dripping purple all the way. "I'll drop it by the Worseleys' on my way to Shiloh."

Margaret set her cup down with a clatter. "Dan, Julie and the kids is coming. I thought they'd be here for lunch.

Besides, the Worseleys will have plenty without my little bit of sweetening."

"Yours. Yours?" He scraped the plate with the side of his fork. The noise set Margaret's teeth on edge. "Who paid for the butter and eggs that went into this cake? You?"

Margaret made herself get up from the table, take two saucers from the stack in the cupboard, cut two slices of cake, and still not look at him.

"Well," she said slowly. "It's my preserves on top. That damson tree came from my daddy's place. I brought it here and set it out myself. You can take the cake." She slid it back toward the center of the table. "But I'll scrape the preserves off first."

For a moment he looked like he had bitten down on something hard. Then he pushed his chair back, letting the legs scratch loudly, and left the room.

Margaret took a bite of cake, got strangled, and coughed until her face was flushed. Then she laughed. "Eat your cake, honey, he ain't taking it nowhere."

In the next room they could hear papers rattling, books slammed shut, and the hoarse voice of the zipper on his old Bible.

"Laura," he yelled. "Come say your verses. You'll be gone when I get back."

Margaret nodded and began to stack the dishes, prompting in a whisper, "Make a joyful noise . . ." She cupped clean plates over the bowls of leftover food, pushed them together, and spread a clean, white cloth over it all like some lumpy corpse.

As she poured water from the kettle into the dishpan she could hear Laura's small voice, "I shall not want. He maketh me . . ."

Margaret moved her lips with the words. When she finished the dishes she opened the back door and dashed out the dishwater in a stream that beaded on the dry ground. Used to have chickens scatter when I'd do that; squawk like a hawk was after 'em. And eggs. I had as many as five dozen a week to sell till the hens quit laying and he wouldn't bring me no biddies from town. Said they was too much trouble. Not to him—he never touched them. Just didn't want me to have that little bit of pleasure.

"Endureth forever." Margaret heard Laura finish. Then his voice and Laura's, talking, but she couldn't catch the words. She dried her hands and waited for Laura to run in, showing her prize.

Instead Laura rushed in, grabbed her grandmother, and wrapped her face in the apron, sobbing in jerks and gasps.

"What's wrong, Lauralee?" Margaret wiped Laura's chin with the apron. "Hush now, you didn't mess up, did you?"

"He says I didn't say it right." Laura's voice shook, she hiccuped. "But I did, Maw Maw, I didn't miss a word."

Margaret rocked her back and forth, cooing. "Hush now, hush." Laura's sobs stopped and the ache in Margaret's chest felt like an open hole. She settled Laura in a chair, pulled her dress over her knees and patted her leg. "What did you mess up on? Which one? We'll say it real quick and you can go try again."

Laura brushed her hand away from her face. "That's what I'm trying to tell you. I said every word right and he said it was still wrong. He said I left out the selahs."

Margaret hugged the child to her, "You just be still, I'll go talk to him."

He was bent over his writing table, the big pen scratching across the page.

"Daniel," she said and he didn't stop. "Daniel, why don't you give the child the gold piece like you promised? It's breaking her heart."

He laid the pen down slowly and began to fumble with the gold chain below his belt. The five-dollar gold piece dangled a small clinking sound. His voice was firm, distinct. "I told her, and you heard me, Margaret," he looked at his watch, snapped the lid shut and slid it into the small slot in his pants. "I told her she couldn't miss a word, not one—if she did, I'd not give her the gold piece."

"I know what you said"—Margaret's voice was controlled—"and she didn't miss a word. She said them perfectly before dinner."

He curled his lips slightly, "With the selahs?"

"Not with the selahs, no. They're not in my Bible and that's the one I taught her out of. They're not part of it anyway. You can't count that." Margaret's cheeks felt hot. "You're not going to disappoint that child. You hear me!" She turned to go.

"What do you think you'll do about it?"

He was holding his position and Margaret shook. "I don't know." She was mad enough to cry. Papa always said I was tenderhearted and Daniel knows it. Treat his family like dogs and go around so mealy-mouthed. People saying what a good man Preacher Rivers is. "For all I care you can take that cake to those good-for-nothing Worseleys," she snapped.

"Fine," he said, as though the word tasted good in his mouth—"I'll do it. But that won't get you the gold piece."

"You don't care how you hurt people, do you?" She pushed her hair back, felt for a loose tendril, and jabbed it in place with a u-shaped pin.

"I'll give her the gold piece on one condition," he said quietly.

Margaret waited.

"I'll give Laura the gold piece if"—he paused, and still she did not turn to face him—"if you give five dollars to the church."

"Five dollars." She sputtered out the words. "From the money my daddy left me? I meant not one red cent of that was ever going to the church. It was for me and my children. What did that church ever do for me. Snicker behind my back, compare me to Lily. Nobody ever lived as perfect as they made her out to be. Keep your old gold piece. Let them bury you with it on." She said it and she was glad. She stalked out of the room, floors popping under wide, flat heels.

"Come on," she said to the frightened Laura, who jumped

from the chair, her face white patches in red. "We'll find something better than his old gold piece if he wants to be that way."

"What?" Laura said as they went out the door, around the house to the porch and to the swing. "What, Maw Maw?"

Margaret leaned back, closed her eyes, and swung back and forth. Fast at first, then slower, the chains alternately crying and grunting.

"What can I have, Maw Maw?"

Margaret didn't answer and Laura snuggled close. "I meant for that money not to be touched till I was dead and gone. Papa left it to me and my children. They never had much all these years and I never touched that money but once and that was to buy this swing." She pulled Laura's dark head into her lap. She was warm and sleepy. Precious child. I never had time to hold Mary much when she was little. Always had work waiting on me, never finished.

Laura snored once, her eyelids twitched and Margaret rocked the swing back and forth gently. What will I give this child? She worked so hard, and it's my fault for not teaching her out of his old pulpit Bible. But he would have found something to keep from giving her that gold piece no matter what I did. Had her heart set on it and what can I give her in its place? Everything pretty I had wore out long ago, or got lost, or give away. The things the children send, she wouldn't want.

Margaret leaned back and stared at the rusty chain, followed it up as far as her fingers would reach toward the fly speckled ceiling. Got to take the swing down soon, put it away for the winter. Put the chains back in the oil cans to keep 'em from rusting. Can't leave it out in the weather, old as it is, wouldn't last no time. She sighed. Gettin' too old to be climbing in and out of that barn loft with this swing. Every year I'm scared I'll fall—break my leg.

"Laura." She shook the child gently. "Honey, I know what you can have." Laura didn't open her eyes, just wiggled closer to Margaret and slept on.

Margaret gave a push with her foot, it bumped a raised board in the floor and the swing jiggled, then was smooth. She drifted back and forth, lifted her feet and coasted. I want to remember how it feels for a long time. I've always liked a swing.

The Wreath-Ribbon Quilt

WE SIT WAITING for Christmas, strangers whose lives are linked by blood, marriage, and memories. This is a rare calm. From the living room my daughters' voices float in a kind of music as they giggle and talk, shake packages and bells.

My brother Gary, tall in his blue V-neck sweater, flips channels on television, a montage of people, snow scenes, disasters, and commercials on digestion aids. The first year Gary went off to college it seemed he grew like a hollyhock. At his wedding I noticed for the first time he was taller than Daddy. Gary's wife, Anne, sits in the Boston rocker and feeds their six-month-old baby. Bubbles in her bottle float to the top, work like yeast.

Beside me on the sofa, Henry, my husband, leafs through an ancient issue of *Reader's Digest*. The corners are so curled he must press them flat to read, "I am Joe's Heart."

This lull is strange. Not peaceful, for there is a touch of tension present, but for the first time in days, I begin to relax. No cookies to roll, cut, and sugar-sprinkle, no gifts to wrap, ribbons to fluff and tie; my hands, not in motion, lie like clay birds in a nest behind my knees.

My father's chair is empty. A blue plastic recliner, it looms large, casts a square shadow in the corner.

Mother bangs a spoon in the kitchen stirring oyster stew. We always have oyster stew on Christmas Eve, but before, Daddy in a red striped apron, arms at angles like airplane wings, tasted and stirred. He heated it slowly, peppered, paprikaed twice, made us wait until he pronounced the thick broth creamy-perfect.

Gary, on the sofa now, moves an embroidered pillow, sits beside Henry. They discuss the Superbowl, who's to win. Their talk turns to cars and Gary moans the loss of the sweet sports car he traded for Anne's station wagon.

"I could feel it," Anne says quickly. "He used to scare me half to death. Could have killed us both trying to see how much that car would do. I told him to either drive with sense or let me out. God, he tried to fly the thing."

My legs prickle under me and the sofa becomes a plush automobile seat. Daddy makes the speedometer needle move from 80 to 90 and past. My mother screams, "What are you trying to do? Kill us all? Make the car fly? Stop and let me out. You can kill yourself if you want to, but let me and the baby out." I watched the needle ease slowly back; the trees become trees out of the green fuzzy blur. The wind noise stops and my father, not laughing any longer, is angry, his face red as strawberry cake. Mother lets her breath out slowly and loud. My legs relax against the seat.

Mother comes from the kitchen, wipes her hands on her white apron, and pushes a footstool near Anne and the baby. She pats the baby's pink-knitted-bootie feet. "I'm surprised she can still wear these. She's growing so fast."

The baby smiles. Milk trickles from the corner of her mouth and down her hill of a chin. "If you don't want the rest of this—" Anne holds the bottle up. The baby reaches out a starfish hand, settles quickly back.

"I haven't made oyster stew in so long." Mother pushes

back her hair. "I didn't know if I would remember how . . . and the only oysters I could find seemed small."

I used to fish oysters, large as shells, lift them from my bowl to Daddy's. He'd make some joke about lead in his pencil.

My daughters run in from the living room and swing onto Henry's lap. Jackie hugs his neck, whispers loudly toward his ear, "Can't we open just *one* present now?"

Henry glances at me. "No, let's wait. It won't be much longer." He tickles her stomach and she folds up laughing. Kate joins them in the horseplay.

I remember Daddy teasing me, making me wait, the suspense and surprise a mixture of aching delight. Now Christmas seems a whirlwind of duties, demands. Even the gifts we give and get are practical: pajamas and robes, toaster-ovens and fry pans. Last year I gave Gary, as a joke, a book, "Making Wine at Home." Anne told me later the only thing they got was a jug of the darkest vinegar and a stain the size of a dinner plate on their kitchen ceiling.

Daddy used to make wine. I wonder if Gary remembers. Daddy made it before there were books on the subject, before wine-making was a fad kind of thing to do. He had wooden kegs in the basement and the air smelled purple, later a fuzzy gray. His wine, like Gary's, failed. He rolled kegs onto the grass, removed the plugs, let dark liquid, the color of blood, gush over othe green lawn. Mother came out to ask if it would hurt the grass. Daddy didn't answer.

One of the girls, Jackie, whines at Henry's elbow, "I don't see why we can't open one present now."

Henry says after we eat they can open all the presents. Mother says if they don't stop fussing, Santa Claus will hear them and not bring the Teresa Tresses dolls they want.

They never saw my father as Santa Claus. The suit he rented sagged and bunched under the wide, black plastic belt. His curled beard could have covered two chins. After a drink or two at each of the first dozen homes Daddy visited, stomping snow from his boots and ho-hoing louder as the night moved on, he would have to hire someone to drive the car. Gary refused. He said if Daddy wanted to make a fool of himself at his age, he didn't want to be present to see it. When someone brought Daddy home, heavy after midnight, he was dressed in regular clothes. I never knew what happened to the Santa Claus suit.

Mother goes to the closet, rumbles in it. "You can't wait, can you, honey?" She gives the girls a box of toys. There is a rusty wind-up drummer boy Gary used to have. It lies broken on top. Hanging from one corner is a doll I never liked. She is wigless and her scalp a patch of sticky lint.

Kate carries the box to the living room. Mother winks at me. "That should keep them busy a little while. Their minds off opening presents, at least until the stew gets ready."

She pulls a plastic bag from a closet shelf, takes out a rainbow of ribbons. "Do you want these?" She strokes the ribbons, pulls a green one through her fingers.

"What?" I can't think why I would want the ribbons. They are too large for the girls to wear, if they ever wore such things, too limp for bows, too wide for gift wrapping. "Where did you get them?"

"Your father's funeral." She looks surprised that I had to ask. "The wreaths. I took them off the wreaths." She lays ribbons in a row down her arm. "They've been washed and pressed."

My head aches from the smell of carnations. A room filled and hot with carnations.

"You can make a coverlet," Mother says. "I've seen some beautiful ones. All ribbons of the same colors can be a border, others worked into a pattern."

I see Mother pluck bows from each wreath, gathering her arms full like a garden bouquet. "No." I shake my head. "No."

She's disappointed. I think of the hours she's spent unwinding wires, washing ribbons, the work to iron satin without scorching. "There's enough purple ones," she holds several ribbons the color of awards. "They'd make a nice border."

"You keep them. You make a coverlet." I look to Henry for help. He's hiding in his reading. The *Reader's Digest* is desperation. I wish he'd notice what's happening, change the subject, say something, say anything.

Gary holds the baby, Lucinda. He pats her back until she burps loudly. "Atta girl," he says and kisses the top of her head wobbling on its stem of neck.

Anne restacks the diaper bag, folds in a terrycloth bib.

"I thought sure you'd want them." Mother closes the bag, stuffs it back into the closet. Her dress is a Christmas red. She never wore black or navy blue, not even to the funeral.

Ribbons the color of carnations. In my mind I see the wreaths still, my father's frozen face, the scar untouched; not even the undertakers would try to camouflage it. The scar that was a ditch of cuts and bruises, his face a mass of purple and red that night. "Go, you old tomcat, you," my mother screamed at him. He stood, head on his arms resting against the wall like someone being searched. "You got what you deserved," she yelled. "Some woman's husband came home too soon."

Gary, eyes bright with fever, dark hair limp, sat on her lap, hand over his ear. An infection woke him screaming in the night. Mother had been rocking him, I heard him cry, the even *whump, whump* of the rocker, was almost asleep again when Daddy came home and the argument began. Mostly an argument in Mother's voice. I stumbled sleepily into a room of people I knew but did not know. Mother pointed at Daddy, then the door. "Go on," she said. "Don't make me look at the mess you are."

He said something, pried my hands loose, and left. I didn't run after him and for the rest of the night, and several after, kept hearing his returning footsteps that weren't there.

In the weeks he was gone, Mother never used his name. I don't know what she told the neighbors, her friends, Mr. Edwards at the lumber company. If he was missed by anyone but me, if she was worried he wouldn't come back, I didn't know.

He did come back, one night. I came in for breakfast and he was in his place at the table buttering toast, his face healed except for the scar. He didn't look at me and I strangled on my orange juice. Mother came to lift my arm, help me stop coughing, but I ran to the bathroom. Daddy was gone when I got back. "Where's Daddy?"

"Gone to work," she said, and started clearing the table.

Daily routines became routine again, no questions were asked, at least not in my presence, nor explanations given. The scar across Daddy's face stayed dark and ragged the rest of his life.

Mother startles me by slamming the closet door, saying, "I better check the stew. It may be boiling over. Goodness." Then she calls me to set the table.

I arrange crackers in a basket. She says it would be nice if we had some sprigs of artificial pine or holly to tuck in for color.

Jackie, my five-year-old, runs in, holds out a toy. "Look." The toy is a plastic skull the size of a shrunken head.

"Where did you get this?"

"The toy box."

Mother ladles stew. "That thing." She hands me a bowl to put on the table. "I found it in the yard raking leaves. Some child dropped it Halloween."

"It's horrible. Ugly."

"Let's see if it still works." Mother presses a tear-shaped spot on the skull's forehead. Its eyes light red, blink; a harsh, grinding sound begins.

Jackie holds the skull to her ear like a shell. "It's laughing."

The tinnish laughter gets louder, grates on.

My father laughed at death when he watched the speedometer needle rise, when he talked of minefields, buddies blown up in his lap. Nobody dies until their time comes, he said. I worried for years he'd crash in a car, get a shotgun blast in the chest, or be found bloody in somebody else's bed. He died in his chair, newspaper spread across his knees. His reading glasses fell to the floor, dropped but did not crack.

I snatch the screaming skull and throw it like a grenade out the kitchen door.

"Don't let cold air in." Mother puts another bowl of stew on the table. "Let's eat while this is hot."

Lucinda starts to fuss when Anne puts her in the infant seat. She wiggles and waves her arms until I pick her up.

"Go ahead and eat," I tell everyone. "We'll go see the tree."

"Lights," I tell Lucinda. She finds my face more interesting. Eyes that blink and are wet. With a warm finger, she traces silver trickles down my cheeks, laughs. I am holding her tighter than I realize. She squirms to be free.

The Eyes of Argus

AMY BASS HELD the black button on the red sweater with her thumb as she pulled the needle through. "Didn't know whether to use the black or red thread, but white's all you had, so I guess I didn't need to worry in the first place, did I?" She laughed through her nose and it tickled so she rubbed it.

At the ironing board, Mrs. Holly thumped the iron on its heel, jerked off the small brown gingham dress, shook it several times, then laid it back, spreading the collar like a doily. She attacked the collar with the tip of her iron, moving her fingers in the lace just a jump ahead of the iron. There was a small tearing sound like a weak cry and she lifted her iron quickly, frowning. "Snagged a place in that lace." She puckered her mouth as though holding pins. "Guess it's one you missed when you mended."

Amy looked up. "Law, I might have missed one, and more. I was lucky to catch as many as I did. Lace was nothing but hanging threads in some places."

Mrs. Holly worked slower now. "It still makes me mad—

Lou Christen giving us these things the shape they was in."

Mrs. Holly was thin as a post with long stilt-like legs, dangling arms, and large hands. She had quick black eyes that didn't miss a trick and knew everything in the neighborhood before it happened. She often said, "I told you so," and nobody disputed her. Nobody disputed her when she said it was funny the fuel oil man kept stopping at Granny Bakewell's and it hot weather. And a few months later Grovine was going around singing all day and looking like she swallowed a pumpkin seed. That was Eppie; and Eppie had hardly got into the world good when Mrs. Holly saw Peuse Ekins slipping around the neighborhood. She gave him a piece of her mind, but it was too late; Lucille was on her way. That's when Mrs. Holly sat down with Granny and had a long talk and nobody disputed that, either.

Amy fumbled in the tin box in her lap and the buttons made clicking noises as she shuffled. "They aren't going to match."

Mrs. Holly snorted. "Never understood why anybody would go so far as to cut buttons off good clothes." She banged the iron on the board. "Just do the best you can. What does it matter if the buttons don't match, long as it holds the sweater together. It'll be something to keep 'em warm . . . poor little things."

Amy finished the sweater, buttoned it, and held it out. It didn't really look too bad. She had put the black buttons at the bottom, where they wouldn't show so much. She tucked the sweater arms back, folded a neat red square, and laid it on the mound of clothes in four boxes lined against the wall like huge tins of bread dough rising. She and Mrs. Holly had collected all the clothes: dresses, coats, sweaters, pajamas, shoes, even three pairs of galoshes. Mildewed, but after they were wiped and wrapped in brown paper, they looked good. She did hope the rest of the clothes wouldn't pick up that awful, rubbery smell. She unfolded a pair of little girl's panties; fourteen pairs they had in all. Enough to do 'em for a while. Three boxes of things to go to Eppie and Lucille at the orphanage, and the last box was for Grovine. Most of the things in Grovine's box came from Mrs. Holly. Some dresses and a pair of brown oxfords she said "just killed her feet." Amy had put in a purple corduroy robe her children gave her Christmas, six years ago. She liked the robe, but every time she wore it, lint flocked to it like a magnet. "Grovine ought to like that purple robe," she said as she fingered it.

Mrs. Holly plumped a puff sleeve on the brown dress, picked up her iron, then set it back. "Here, Amy, you better do this. I don't know nothing about ironing little girls' things in the first place." She took Amy's chair, wiped long fingers across her forehead, and pushed back tassels of gray hair.

Amy spread the sleeve like a paper muffin cup and wiggled her iron across it. "It's been a while, but I guess you don't forget."

Mrs. Holly rocked. "Somebody has to see to them. If H.C. had been the kind of brother he ought to be to Grovine, we wouldn't have had to take so much on ourselves."

Amy switched to the other sleeve. "It's awful how people—and family at that—can have no more feeling for each other."

"'Course, it was to be expected. He didn't come around them when Granny was alive, and who'd think it now? Remember the funeral."

Amy touched a few places on the collar and nodded, "H.C. on one side of the church, Grovine on the other. If it hadn't been for you and me and John, and the rest of the neighbors, there wouldn't have been a soul setting with poor Grovine."

Mrs. Holly got up and pushed the boxes close together, sighing. "In a way you can't blame him. Grovine with her petticoat showing the whole time. And if I hadn't taken it on myself"—she tapped her finger on her chest—"*myself,* to get those kids ready, no telling how they would have showed up at their own grandma's funeral. Naked as jaybirds, I reckon."

Amy unplugged the iron, looked at the electric clock above the stove. "It's ten o'clock. I didn't know it was that late. John will be wanting his hot milk, says it helps him to sleep. You'd think the way he snores, he wouldn't need it." She laid the iron's cord across the board and it dangled like a cat's tail. "I better be getting towards home."

Mrs. Holly took the brown dress, folded it carefully, and laid it on a box. "We done a good job, if I do say so. And everything's ready to go.

They decided to leave after nine the next morning. Mrs. Holly wanted to miss the mill traffic. Amy wrapped her shawl around her shoulders and darted out the back door, running across two back yards to her own. Her flashlight made zig-zags of light as she ran.

John was already in bed when she got there and after rolling her hair in knots on yellow plastic curlers she ducked her head inside a flannel gown, yanking off her clothes as she pulled down the gown, then curled next to John's back. He did have the hairiest back.

She was asleep before she knew it and dreaming of cherubs in pink feathered pinafores who played flutes and danced. They danced so close their feathers tickled and she laughed. They begged her to dance too and she did, dancing on the lightest feet until the rain started. But it wasn't rain; it was hard drops like crystal candies that stung when they hit. And when the drops hit the street they melted in a hiss. The cherubs cried and started to run, but the street was hot and burned their bare feet. Their cries were still ringing in her ears when she awoke enough to realize the dog was whining to go out.

At breakfast she was tired and John grumped because his newspaper was late and the grits had lumps. She was relieved when he finally left for the store, flinging his jacket across his arm, his hat crooked on his head.

She dressed quickly in her navy blue crepe, her white Enna Jetticks, and got to the driveway just as Mrs. Holly finished loading the boxes in the trunk of her fat black Buick. The Buick had been her husband's before his death twelve years ago, and the paint had worn down to a mottled reddish-brown color.

Amy pulled on her gloves, holding her white purse flat against her stomach. When both gloves were on, she pressed her pancake of a straw hat flatter to her head and walked around the car. She got in, shut the door twice before she was satisfied. Didn't want to take any chances on falling out.

In the driver's seat, Mrs. Holly released the brake and let the car roll down the driveway and into the street before she started the motor. After she raced the motor several times the car jerked up the street, then bounced to a stop in front of a paintless two-story house with a leaning porte cochere. Under a bare chinaberry tree stood a straight chair, its seat torn and dragging the ground, making the new red-and-white "For Sale" sign sparkle in the yard.

"Just hurts me to see that," Mrs. Holly said, sucking in her lip. "But I guess none of us is going to live forever."

Amy folded her hands on her purse in her lap and crossed her ankles. It didn't seem possible. Six months ago Granny would have had the clothesline filled by this time of morning, and Grovine, Eppie, and Lucille out playing playhouse under the tree.

"Such a shock." Mrs. Holly stopped at the traffic light. "Her just to keel over like that. At least Grovine had enough sense to come get me. But you know, that girl wasn't any more excited or worried than if her mama had sent her over to borrow a cup of flour. I knew something was wrong when she said Granny was laying in the middle of the kitchen floor. Granny was one woman that didn't stop from sunup to sundown."

"No siree." Amy stared straight ahead. "Didn't stop till she dropped dead in her tracks. Like you and me, I reckon." She laughed and looked at Mrs. Holly in her gray wool suit and black felt hat.

"Well, I hope not." Mrs. Holly stiffened her shoulders. "One of these days I want to sit back and let my younguns wait on me."

"That's right." Amy nodded quickly. "At least our younguns have minds and won't be a burden on us like Grovine was. I said a long time ago she was going to be the death of Granny." She took a handkerchief from her purse and blew her nose loudly, then lowered her voice. "If Grovine had been sent away someplace when she was little . . ."

"I know, I know." Mrs. Holly held the steering wheel tightly, and sighed. "I hated to be the one to call the County on Grovine, but somebody had to. Pitiful the way those girls was running around barefooted and it frost on the ground." She slowed the car, pointed to a neat white house framed by a mat of green lawn. "Look at that. Ethel Shaw's got buttercups blooming already. Mine ain't even come up yet." She twisted her neck and moved her lips as if she were counting the blooms.

"I declare, they sure are pretty." Amy stretched to get a better look. "Ethel always been so smart. Give me two bags of dresses her Sybil had outgrowed, said they ought to fit Eppie, if they didn't she could grow into them. There was a red polka-dotted one, and a—"

"There's Ethel out in her yard now." Mrs. Holly nosed the car across the road and parked facing traffic. A blue truck tooted loudly as it swerved around them. "Yoo-hoo, Ethel," Mrs. Holly yelled as she lowered the window. "Your yard sure does look pretty."

Ethel, in men's striped coveralls, laid her trowel in a tulip bed, dusted dirt from her hands and walked toward the car.

"We're going to the orphanage to take Eppie and Lucille them things we rounded up. You want to go?"

"I'd love to"—Ethel had a dirt streak like a dark scar across her cheek—"but I'm fixing to feed my boxwoods and I need to get it done before they start putting out. You all go on without me this time." She stepped back from the car.

"Sure do thank you for all them dresses." Amy leaned toward the window and hollered.

Ethel nodded. "You're sure welcome. Glad to get shed of them."

Mrs. Holly said, "Amy told me how you did every one of them up, too. Not everybody was that nice." Her tone was cold. "I was up till ten o'clock last night. Lou Christen give me a box of things and I had to wash and iron every one of them myself. Some of 'em was nothing but rags—and she'd cut the buttons off—"

"Lou Christen?" Ethel's face stretched. "I never wouldn've thought it of her. All the money she and Ham's got and her cutting buttons off. They could buy a whole storeload of buttons."

"Now, Ethel, don't let on I said that." Mrs. Holly shifted gears. "I wouldn't want to spread anything. It's what's in a person's heart that counts, I've always said."

Amy wiggled a gloved finger at Ethel as they drove away. When they crossed the center line, a blonde in a red convertible had to screech her tires to avoid hitting them.

"Did you see that hussy?" Mrs. Holly asked. "Bet she keeps the drugstores in business buying peroxide. Nobody's hair's that color naturally."

Amy put her handkerchief in her purse and snapped it shut. "I think we did real well rounding up as many things as we did. And Mr. Andrews at the store giving five dollars for Grovine—"

Mrs. Holly speeded up. "He said give it to her and tell her to buy what she needed, but I'm not handing her money. She wouldn't know what to do with it if she had it. I bought her a slip and three pair of step-ins. They had 'em three pair for a dollar in Belk's basement—seconds, but she won't know the difference."

As they passed the old Pickens place Amy fussed about how it had run down since old man Pickens died and his children fighting to keep one from getting a cent more than another. When they passed the Weatherfords' new house, Mrs. Holly said she had heard there was a bathroom for every bedroom and could remember when John Weatherford was knee-high to a grasshopper and didn't have a rag to wipe his nose on.

"You never hear of him going out of his way to do nothing for nobody," Mrs. Holly said angrily.

"Must be kin to H.C.," Amy shot back, and they both laughed.

They rode in silence when the road became familiar. Finally Amy said, "One good thing about it, the county sure didn't waste any time getting those kids taken into the home, and Grovine settled too."

"She won't last." Mrs. Holly shook her head. "Somebody'll have to tell her every step to make."

"I know it." Amy swallowed loudly. "And then what'll happen to her? And what do you reckon will be done with the money from the sale of Granny's house? You think H.C. will stick it in his pocket and Grovine not get a thing from her own mama's estate?"

"Lord, it's no telling what's going on. If Grovine can just hold out to work I'll feel better. And knowing Eppie and Lucille is being taken care of is a load off my mind. That orphanage may not be the fanciest place in this world, but they'll be raised right. There's a church there, I heard, and the kids march in every day for chapel and twice on Sunday."

"Is it an orphanage for girls, or girls and boys both?"

"Both, I heard, but I think the boys' home is on the other side of the road and somebody said they even have separate dining halls." Mrs. Holly squinted. "What's that sign say? Tillman's Home?"

"Tillman's Home for Orphan Children," Amy said proudly. "This is it."

Mrs. Holly steered the car toward the center of the brick-pillared entrance with a series of short pulls, tugs, and audible grunts. "Which one of those buildings do you think they'll be in?"

They parked on the grass in front of the first brick building, under a large oak tree. Mrs. Holly got out, looked at the gray sky, held her hand palm up and said "Sure looks like rain" to a large dark cloud.

Amy waited at the car trunk until Mrs. Holly took her elbow, leaned close, and said, "We'll leave the clothes and things in the car and surprise them later. Poor little things, aren't they going to be tickled?"

Amy patted her purse. "I had John bring them some penny candy from the store . . . little younguns need a bit of sweetening once in a while. You don't think they'll take it away from them, do you?"

"Naw." Mrs. Holly breathed hard and grabbed the wrought iron rail beside the brick steps.

Amy pushed the wooden door and waited as Mrs. Holly sailed mightily through. "Well." She stood inside and looked around. "You can say one thing. This place sure is clean." She smiled and whispered to Mrs. Holly, "Just like a living room. They got reading lamps, a rug, and even a television set."

Mrs. Holly marched to the desk, holding her purse to her chest like a shield. "We'd like to see Eppie and Lucille Bakewell, please."

The lady in the pink blouse smiled, handed her a card and pencil. "Just complete this form while I call them. Are you expected?"

Mrs. Holly turned to Amy and said, "Don't see why I have to fill out any card—I'm just visiting—not wanting to adopt them."

"It's routine," the girl said, still smiling. "For our records."

"Very well." Mrs. Holly wrote her name large, the H straight and stiff. She was still writing when the lady behind the desk sang out, "Here's our Eppie and Lucy. You girls have company, isn't that nice?"

Like a color snapshot, Eppie and Lucy stood in the doorway, side by side, holding hands. Eppie, the seven-year-old, had her hair in a neat brown pageboy with bangs, and her red plaid pinafore was crisp and new-looking. Lucille, her blonde ringlets topped by a bow, pulled at the lace collar on her blue dress and stood with one toe of her black patent shoes against the floor. There *was* lace on her blue socks.

"My goodness." Mrs. Holly went to them. "You girls must have known we was coming and got all dressed up."

"No, ma'am." Eppie didn't smile.

Lucille dropped Eppie's hand and grinned.

"They must be feeding you girls good up here." Amy pinched Lucille's pink cheek. It was warm, smooth as cream.

"Oh, yes," Lucille said. "We had strawberry shortcakes last night and today we're having—"

Mrs. Holly frowned tight bands across her forehead.

"Eppie," the lady behind the desk said, "why don't you girls take the ladies to see your room? Then show them around the grounds."

"Yes, ma'am." Eppie turned and started down the hall.

Lucille took Amy's hand and Mrs. Holly followed.

"It's room twelve," Lucille said, skipping beside Amy, her head bobbing like a buoy. "We can see the lake from my window, and Joanne, she's my best friend, says in the summer we get to go swimming and have hot dog roasts and—"

"That's fine . . . just fine," Amy panted.

Eppie went inside a door at the end of the hall and Lucille led in Amy.

When Mrs. Holly got to the room she stuck in her head like an old turtle and muttered, "This sure is nice . . . nice."

Amy sat on one of the hobnail bedspreads on a maple twin bed and Eppie sat at one of the desks on each side of the window.

"We can't stay." Mrs. Holly stood rooted, like a large potted plant, in the hall.

"Just for a minute," Amy said, and patted Lucille's leg. "We wanted to see how you girls was getting along." She picked at a tuft on the spread. She'd been saving stamps to get one just like it and only needed three-fourths of a book more. "Do you like it here?" She untied Lucille's bow and retied it, crookedly.

Lucille bounced on the bed beside her. "Oh, yes, Mrs. Adams, my teacher is so sweet and I go to kindergarten. I drew these." She pointed to the pictures on the wall.

"You ever see your mother?" Mrs. Holly inched inside the room.

"Yes, ma'am. Mr. Ervin brings her every Sunday."

"Mr. Ervin?" Mrs. Holly's eyebrows shot up as though someone had pressed a spring.

"Yes, ma'am." Eppie turned the pages of a book on her desk.

"He brings us candy," Lucille chirped, "a whole box and we can give some to our friends."

Amy pulled the two little brown paper bags from her purse. "I was about to forget to give you girls this. My memory's no longer than a minute. I'd forget my head if it wasn't fastened to me."

Eppie peeped inside her bag, squeezed it shut, and set it at the back of her desk.

Lucille ran her hand into her bag, pulled out a pinkish square, and said, "Is it peppermint? I don't like peppermint." She shut her bag and handed it to Eppie.

"Well, my goodness." Mrs. Holly's face was flushed. "You can certainly give it to someone and not let it go to waste." She stared hard at the closet door. "Do you all have plenty to wear—or is what you got on all you have?"

"Oh, no." Lucille ran to the closet. "We got lots of dresses. The first day we went to Wardrobe and they let us pick out what we wanted." She flung the closet door wide, revealing two neat rainbows of dresses.

Mrs. Holly turned, one foot in the hallway as if she were getting set on her mark. "I guess we better be going."

"But we haven't—" Amy stood, stretched her arm after Mrs. Holly. "Wait, we got all those things in the car yet—" She turned to Lucille. All the work she and Mrs. Holly had done, surely . . . "Honey, does everybody up here have as many dresses as you do?"

"Oh, no," Lucille said, "they got more 'cause they been here longer."

Eppie gave them a cold look and went back to her book.

"We'll see you girls again," Amy said from the hall.

Lucille dashed after them. "We didn't show you the cafeteria or the library, or—"

"We'll go next time, honey." Amy patted Lucille's shining hair.

The girls sure did look good. She hurried after Mrs. Holly. She'd never thought Eppie was pretty. Her forehead was too broad, but with bangs . . .

As she passed the desk, the lady in the pink blouse sang out, "You ladies come again. We'd love to have you any time."

Mrs. Holly drew in her breath as she marched past, but Amy smiled and waved.

Mrs. Holly went down the steps faster than she'd come up them and left Amy to close the door. In the car she started the motor and was backing before Amy got settled.

"Wait," Amy said, "I got my dress-tail caught. I was in such a hurry—wait." She opened the door, pulled her dress in and held a corner of it in her lap, brushing it. "Hope I didn't get any grease on it." She banged her door shut. "Grease is so hard to get out."

"My doors don't have grease on them," Mrs. Holly said flatly.

Amy leaned back, her dress spread across her knees. "What are we going to do with all those—?"

Mrs. Holly didn't answer, just looked in her rearview mirror, her lips clamped together.

"This isn't the way we came, is it?" Amy said as they turned onto a dirt road.

"No," Mrs. Holly slowed down. "Look at that dust boil up . . . whew. At the county they said this is the quickest way to the place where Grovine's staying . . . They could've told me it wasn't paved."

"Six months." Amy played with the handles of her purse. "It's just been six months since Eppie and Lucille was taken to the home. I never thought I'd see such a difference in those younguns. Looka yonder"—she pointed to a large windmill near a barn. "You reckon them things really work or are they just for looks?"

Mrs. Holly glanced at the windmill quickly, then went back to reading names on mailboxes. "White Oak Farm,

Hope Crest Farms, Four Pines, Treetops is the one we want . . ."

"Treetops," Amy said excitedly. "Right there. On that big mailbox."

Mrs. Holly saw nothing but another dusty road and trees. "Can't see the house for the trees," she muttered. They crossed a creek, the car jouncing on a wooden bridge, then up a hill. "Hope we don't meet anything. This road isn't wide enough to pass a cat. Don't see why anybody ever—"

They rounded the curve and saw the house for the first time, a gleaming white house with four large columns across the front. "Law, it looks like something out of a picture, don't it?" Amy craned her neck and pressed her nose against the cool windshield. Beyond the house she could see rows of gleaming metal chickenhouses like huge bars of silver in the sun. "Wonder if Grovine works in the house or with the chickens? She ought to do real good at gathering eggs."

Mrs. Holly stopped the car and turned off the motor. "I'll see if anybody's home," she said, her hand on the door handle. "They might not want us visiting Grovine during the week. Some places is funny about their help."

Amy watched as Mrs. Holly wiped her feet and walked across the neat flagstone porch. In a moment, the big front door opened and she turned, beckoned Amy to come on. She swung her arm wide as if she were gathering a bundle of air.

Amy left her purse and gloves on the seat, then took her purse, leaving the gloves. You never know who might walk by and decide to help themselves.

Grovine and Mrs. Holly waited as Amy crossed the porch. "You sure do look good, Grovine, honey, real good." She hurried toward them. "Why you used to be nothing but skin and bones . . . A big gust of wind could've blowed you away."

Grovine laughed and put her hand over her mouth. "You all come to see me way out here?" She twisted her terrycloth apron, wringing it like wet wash, then let it go. It twirled against her like a drill and Grovine caught it with both hands, then started flapping it. "You all come to see me!"

"Of course we did, Grovine." Mrs. Holly's voice was soft, sweet, as she patted Grovine's arm, and walked to the white brocade sofa.

"This is the *nicest* house, Grovine." Amy took a seat beside Mrs. Holly. "Everything's so fancy." She ran her hand over the shiny coffee table.

Grovine smiled, making a church steeple with her fingers.

"It sure is," Mrs. Holly echoed.

The sun poured through stiff organdy curtains and made a rainbow on the cut glass vase on the marble mantel. "You keep everything this clean?" Mrs. Holly glanced around. "Must be a big job."

"Yes'um," Grovine lifted her chin. "I dust in here and Matildabelle runs the sweeper and waxes and—"

"Matildabelle? Is that Mrs. Ervin?"

"Oh, no," Grovine giggled, cupping her hands over her mouth. "Matildabelle's the maid. Mrs. Ervin's been in bed three years. Don't have no use at all for her legs."

"You have to lift and do for her?"

"Oh, no, ma'am." Grovine pulled her hair and held it behind her neck.

"Lifting a sick person—if they're any count at all—will just kill you. Grovine, you can't hold out to do that kind of work and they shouldn't expect you to. Should they, Amy?"

"Oh, no." Amy stopped admiring the ornate gold-rimmed mirror above the mantel. She'd seen pictures in magazines of rooms like this. "It's just too hard on your back."

"I don't do things like that." Grovine stuck out her chin. "Mr. Ervin does. I mainly straighten up her room, and pick some flowers for her, and comb her hair . . ." She looked at her hands in her lap. "I do some of the cooking, but Mr. Ervin helps me with that too."

"Well." Mrs. Holly let out her breath. "I'm glad about that. And he pays you too, does he? Along with your room and board?"

"Oh, yes." Grovine's cheeks looked pinker than ever. "And he's so good to me."

"You're fixing your hair different." Amy said excitedly. "I knew there was something new about you."

"And you've gained weight," Mrs. Holly smiled.

"Yes, ma'am." Grovine blushed.

"Guess you have plenty of milk and eggs, fresh things from the garden, living on a farm." Mrs. Holly picked up a magazine from the table. There was a woman with a low-cut dress on the cover, and big red letters said, "My Husband Is Not My Lover." Mrs. Holly began to fan with it.

"All you can eat, I guess," Amy laughed.

"Well, Eppie and Lucille are doing just fine." Mrs. Holly fanned harder. "We went there first."

Grovine crossed her legs and swung her foot in its trim black shoe with the big gold buckle on the toe. Amy thought of the lace-up brown oxfords in the box. "Eppie and Lucille look so pretty," she breathed.

"Is H.C. doing anything to help you out?" Mrs. Holly's black eyes pinpointed Grovine.

"He got me this job," Grovine said quickly, jumping up. "And that's the best thing ever happened to me. H.C. just leaves me alone, and that's the way I like it." She glared at them, her nostrils enlarged slightly.

"I guess we better be on our way." Amy poked Mrs. Holly with her elbow. "Grovine's probably got things to do."

Grovine held the door for them, wiggling it back and forth, her feet doing little dance steps. "Bye," she said, "bye."

Mrs. Holly fumbled her keys in the ignition, started the motor, then rolled the window down and leaned out. "You make Mr. Ervin bring you to see us now. You hear?"

Grovine had already shut the door.

"Well," Mrs. Holly said, "I guess she didn't hear me." She watched the rearview mirror as she backed. "Keep an eye on that big tree over there, will you? Let me know if I get too close."

"You're okay," Amy said just before they heard the scrape of metal.

Mrs. Holly jammed on the brakes and turned to Amy, her lips in a hard line, eyes snapping. Then she got out with a rush.

Amy held her purse and looked at the house. "Imagine Grovine living in a place like that. Just imagine."

Mrs. Holly got in the car and shifted gears. "It tapped the bumper, but didn't dent it—sure was lucky. Could have been worse. I thought you was watching," she fussed. "I told you to."

Amy didn't say anything and they drove in silence for a while until Mrs. Holly leaned back in her seat and said, "Grovine looked the best I've seen her, didn't you think so?"

"Right fleshy.," Amy took off her hat and laid it in her lap.

A car zoomed around them and Mrs. Holly blew her horn. "Smart-aleck. They ought to keep people like that off the roads. Let them go to the racetracks if they want to race."

"I don't think all that weight was Grovine." Amy slapped her gloves back and forth on her purse.

"What was it then?" Mrs. Holly turned to her.

"You know."

"I know what?"

"You know . . . like before. She always did start to show early."

"You don't reckon?" Mrs. Holly's lower lip dropped and her mouth stayed open for a good two minutes. Amy was about to say if she didn't soon close it, the bugs was going to fly in, but she didn't.

"Who?—How would anything like that happen? Out there on a farm she don't see nobody but Mr. Ervin . . ." The car veered off the road and Mrs. Holly jerked it back. "Mr. Ervin!" she swallowed loudly. "And his wife right there in the same house?" Mrs. Holly clung to the steering wheel. "Oh my . . . oh."

Amy nodded. "I'd bet my life on it." For once she had beat Mrs. Holly to it and it felt good.

"Well." Mrs. Holly stared straight ahead. "It's H.C.'s fault and he can just see to this. He got her the job and got her into the mess. I'm going to write him and dump the whole thing in lap."

Mrs. Holly spluttered and Amy half-listened all the way home. When they turned the corner, she heard the boxes slide in the trunk and couldn't help smiling.

Ethel Shaw, pruning her Crimson Glory rosebushes along the fence, waved as they passed, but Mrs. Holly acted like she didn't even see her, just sped up.

Knotty

THROUGH THE SAVE Mart plate glass window, Beryl saw a shadow dart between a row of parked cars. "Fay," she said to the girl at the next register, "he's still out there."

Neon lightning flashed. *Red, green, blue* . . . would he try to get in her car? It was locked, wasn't it? Lately she locked everything. Would he try to kill her? *Yellow, red* . . . maybe now he was aiming a rifle over her fender. Glass would shatter, people scream and she would be shot . . . killed. Dead. Oh God. She ducked, squatted, pretending to straighten her paper bag file. He couldn't see her now. Knotty, she wanted to scream. Knotty.

Her fingers stuck to the bags. She crushed, wrinkled, rather than straightened them. Their irregular edges looked barbed, menacing.

"You're crazy," she said to herself. "Downright nutty." Of course Knotty would not shoot. No, never anything so noisy. He hated noise. That was one of the things they shared. Hours in bed listening to everything around them. Silence in their own warm world. The fish mouths they made kissing . . . Beryl clamped her hand over her mouth, felt her cold, dry lips.

Fay's register rang, the drawer jangled open, and she clinked change into the customer's hand—a bald man with a bug-like mole on his cheek. He counted with Fay, moving his lips, "Ninety-nine, one dollar."

Beryl whispered loudly to Fay's green smocked back, "What am I going to *do*?"

"Thank you for shopping Save Mart," Fay said to the customer. She shrugged her shoulders and turned to Beryl, "What *can* you do?"

Fay had a long face, hair rippling to her waist and fanning across broad hips. The original Plain Jane, Knotty called her. He used to pull his chin down, mock her. Beryl had laughed, spilled beer on her robe.

"I don't know." Beryl watched the parking lot. Cars left, winking their tails like fireflies. Was Knotty curled in her car? Back seat? He would hide, spring on her, wrap a scarf around her neck, and pull, pull, pull. A scarf was quiet. Her throat felt dry and tight. She needed a drink of water. Never leave the register unattended, Rule Number One in the book of Save Mart. Sometimes Beryl felt chained to that damn register like an organ grinder's monkey.

"Are you going to ring me up, or not?" a fat lady in black stretch pants snapped. Riding her hip like some deformity, a moon-faced child kicked the counter with dirty, bare feet.

"I'm sorry." Beryl cleared her register, picked a pink girdle from the pile of goods and read, "Six eighty-eight, lingerie . . ." The pricetag pin jabbed Beryl's finger and a drop of blood burbled. "Ouch." Beryl put her finger in her mouth, sucked. Blood tasted rusty.

"Don't bleed on my girdle." The woman snatched it up, laid it carefully out of the way. "Don't want it messed up. I ain't even got it home from the store yet."

Beryl punched seventy-nine cents for a can of motor oil. Her finger stopped bleeding, but it looked pale and drained on the tip. "Socks, ladies' socks." She hunted for the department fifty-seven key. Slow tonight, her fingers would not work. "White cotton socks." Knotty wore white cotton socks. She washed them. Maybe he was out there now wearing socks she had washed. No, it had been two weeks since . . .

Beryl picked up a package of training pants. "Eighty-eight cents," she said. The pants in assorted colors, tight under their plastic wrap, looked like rolls of pastel mints.

The woman shifted the child on her hip. "Two years old," she said, "and he ain't broke from wetting his pants."

Beryl rang up a red-handled spatula. "Forty-nine cents." Then a hairbrush. She couldn't find the price sticker, turned it over, looked on the back. The bristles bit her hand and a chill crawled down her back.

"They're a dollar eighty-six," the woman said, "on special. I thought they was a real good buy."

"Yes." Beryl's hand shook as she fingered the keys. "I need a brush. Mine's broken." Knotty broke the handle after he held and scrubbed her with it. Laughing, at first she laughed. Then he wouldn't stop. Her skin burned for days, there were scabs. He was gone for a week after that and she had gotten used to being alone when came back.

"I thought that was a good buy." The woman smiled. There was a large gap between her two front teeth, her eyes were large, rimmed with brown like a raccoon.

Knotty had small darting eyes. Kin to a squirrel, he used to laugh. Fast on my feet.

Beryl picked up a sticky package of marshmallow peanuts. Several rolled onto the counter. She put them back, twisted the bag shut, and gave it to the boy. "Thirty-three," she rang on the register.

"Now you got your candy." The woman jiggled the child. "See, I told you, you'd get it back after the lady rang it up. You happy now?"

The child stuffed both chipmunk cheeks. Orange drool dripped down his bare belly.

"That's a total of twelve seventy-two, including tax,"

Beryl said. She slipped the items into a paper sack, glanced toward the parking lot. Dark, it was too dark to see anyone out there now.

"Thank-you-for-shopping-Save-Mart." She shut her register, leaned upon it. The register was warm, like something alive.

Beryl watched the double doors swing open, the woman hitch the child higher on her hip, clutch her package tight to her chest and sway out, the child dangling like a doll.

"Fay?" Beryl whispered. "You think he's gone?"

"Could be." Fay peeled a stick of gum, folded it into her mouth. "He's your problem, not mine."

At first Fay had liked Knotty, kidded with him. After he moved in with Beryl, she acted different. Jealous, Knotty said. You got a boyfriend and she hasn't. Never will have unless she learns to loosen up a lot.

"Attention all shoppers," the sound system boomed.

Fay gave her mock salute. Beryl usually laughed, but tonight she stood on tiptoes, surveyed the store. Not much of a crowd.

"Save Mart will close in ten minutes. Please make your purchases now."

The lights dimmed, brightened.

I could stay here all night, Beryl thought. Not go to the car, not go home. I'd sleep in the linen department. "Ha," she wanted to say. That fluffy-looking display bed was plywood and hollow underneath. Knotty hid under it the day the police came. The last time she had seen him.

"How can they expect a body to get her shopping done?" A thin lady in a faded floral dress pushed her cart beside the register. "If they turn the lights off and you can't see the price of nothing."

Beryl rang up a flyswatter, some knitting yarn, and a box of chocolate-covered raisins. The woman saw the total and put back the flyswatter, and Beryl had to void the ticket, ring everything again.

Fay locked her register, threw her smock across the bath oil display.

Beryl penciled figures on a sheet.

"Hurry," Fay said, stamping her red-sneakered feet, "these dogs are killing me."

Beryl erased, wrote in another figure. Knotty is going to kill me. He thinks I called the police, that I put them on to him, but I didn't. I didn't.

Knotty bought things at Save Mart. Beryl rang them cheaper. When he returned them for a refund, he got the marked price. At night they giggled, made up stories. Reasons For Refund, they called them. Nothing as simple as "too large," or "too small," but things like, "The dog barked at me when I wore it." Or, "This color clashed with my favorite nail polish." Silly, silly things.

"Come on." Fay lifted one leg like a flamingo.

"Do you see him?" Beryl counted change. Knotty never needed money from "the game." They had her pay and his macramé sales. But he got bored with all those strings and knots and loops that became belts and bags. It was more string and belts and bags, wall hangings—he got bored with it all. Had he been bored with her too?

Fay cupped her hands, pressed her face to the glass. "Not a creature was stirring," she laughed, "not even a mouse."

Beryl shut her drawer, handed the brown drawstring bag and sales sheet to Lorita Willis. "Machines," said Lorita, glancing over her shoulder for Mr. Phelps. "He thinks we're machines that don't have aches or pains or feelings."

Mr. Phelps pranced by. Lorita jerked the bag shut and swished off. He held the door, jangled his keys like a jailer. "Good night, girls," he called. "See you tomorrow."

Humpty Dumpty, Fay called him behind his back. Round, he bounced when he walked.

Two checkout girls filed past him numbly. "Tomorrow's another day," he sang, wiping his shiny forehead with a monogrammed handkerchief. The ring on his little finger caught the light and flashed meanly.

"Another day," Fay said outside, "another dollar—for him."

The lights in the parking lot went off almost immediately. Only neon lit the area. *Red. Blue. Green.* S . . . A . . . V . . . E.

Beryl looked at her VW alone in the back row, listened and heard nothing. Knotty never made noise.

Fay waited for Beryl to unlock her door. "Every customer I had today was a pure, capital B, Bitch." Fay rubbed her feet together. "Do you know what one customer had me do?"

Beryl looked behind the front seat. Only an empty Cheerwine bottle and some popcorn puffs from the last drive-in movie she and Knotty had seen. What was it? Who starred in it? If someone held a gun to her head and said remember, she couldn't. Numb, my head is numb, she thought.

"This one customer"—Fay popped Spearmint—"had the nerve to ask me to open a bag of cookies so she could count to be sure it was 'the exact figure stated on the label'."

Beryl locked the car door, leaned back, and took a deep breath.

"Say," said Fay, "you *are* in a state, huh?"

Berly nodded, started the car, and headed down the boulevard.

"I'm so tired." Fay stretched. "I feel like digging a hole somewhere and crawling in it."

Is that what Knotty would do? Dig a hole and bury her? "Fay?"

"Yeah," said Fay, chewing rapidly. "You want to stay with us?"

Beryl braked for a light. "No . . ." That stuffy house that smelled of mildew and death—those old people. "No, I don't think so." I'll be okay after I get home. Fine.

"You don't seem so shook anymore." Fay drummed on the dash, hummed. "I mean, that might not have been him in the parking lot. Right? It could have been anybody."

"I guess," Beryl said quietly. "Knotty could be a hundred miles away." She let out a little laugh. Maybe it wasn't him. Maybe.

"A thousand miles," said Fay. "You're not still in love—"

"Love? Knotty?" Beryl's throat hurt. "No. Not anymore." Once she loved him, loved him a lot. At first he had been gentle, tender. She had not known . . . waking with him beside her, not being alone anymore . . .

"That's it." Fay swung her purse strap over her shoulder. "Home again. Thanks for the lift."

Beryl parked, let the motor idle. "Night."

Fay blew a tan bubble, pulled it flat with even teeth. "Bye," she said. "See you."

There were lights in Fay's house; people. For a moment Beryl wanted to call, to turn off the car and run up the walk. Fay's mother blocked the light in the doorway. She waved.

Beryl pulled away from the curb. Eight blocks to her apartment. Apartment. That was a joke. Knotty said the house must have been built in 1722 when Mrs. MacCauley was brought there as a bride. Mrs. Mac rented rooms with adjoining closets. Kitchen closet, bathroom closet, bedroom closet.

Beryl parked beside the crepe myrtle hedge. Its wicker limbs wove a fence of shadows along the walk. Mrs. Mac said it was pretty when it bloomed. She wanted a yard full of it.

Beryl locked her car, dropped keys in her purse, and looked up. There was a light in her apartment. A light! One of the small round windows in the eaves glowed. Knotty. Knotty was in her apartment.

She grabbed the car door handle hard and pulled, reached for her keys, then stopped. Where would she go? Fay's? No.

In the empty hallway, Beryl checked her mail. Nothing. Not even an "Occupant" today. How could she expect mail when no one knew where she was?

You left the lamp on, she said to herself, climbing the stairs. Reading the newspaper, you forgot. This morning she was looking for something about Knotty. Two weeks ago she had read on page 11B, "James Null Crowell, released, pending further investigation." She read it a dozen times. There had been nothing since.

On the second floor Beryl paused. Someone in Apartment C was watching TV. They drowned the canned laughter in all the right places. Across the hall, a baby cried and a voice yelled, "Make that kid shut up."

Before she reached the top of the second stairs she saw the light from her apartment and stopped. Oh God, what if Knotty was waiting?

No, she decided. He wouldn't have the light on. Would he?

Her key made a small, sharp click when the lock released. She shoved open the door, stepped back and hugged the hall wall, broken plaster tearing her pantyhose. If you are in there Knotty, come out . . . now.

Nothing.

Beryl peeped around the facing. Her apartment looked as she had left it this morning. Fuzzy slippers on the floor, newspapers sprawled across the sofa, dirty slacks and blouse draped like a corpse across a chair.

She walked in, closed the door and went to the bedroom. "Knotty," she whispered. Under the bed she found a rumpled magazine, an empty tube of lipstick, and some dirty panties. In the shower, the faucet dripped. In one closet she banged hangers and said, "Knotty?"

Finally she sank on the sofa. Knotty was not here. Had not been here in two weeks. She stared at the fly-speckled ceiling, the stain made when the roof leaked. She would relax. Relax until tomorrow when she would have to go through the whole thing again. If he were here, she could deal with him. Yell and scream and throw things. He'd run. But out there—she didn't know. Didn't know how mad he was, if he hated her. Mr. Phelps called the police. Not her. Sometimes she wished she had and told them everything she knew.

She closed her eyes, exhausted, too weak even to cry.

In the next apartment a dog whined to go out.

Someone opened the door, jingled a leash. "Come on, boy," they called, "come on."

If Knotty came back, Beryl thought, it would be like

before. They'd sleep late on Sundays, make love on the *Times* and take turns afterward reading their backsides. They would pour salt on slugs and watch them curl black. They would send Mrs. Mac a plastic funeral wreath for Mother's Day and laugh until they cried. Laugh until she cried.

Sisters under the Skin

THE LIVER-COLORED PONY, four legs spread, lay in the pasture stiff as a carnival horse.

"Lord." Leona nosed the faded blue Plymouth down the road. "If that pony don't look for all the world like he's dead."

Her sister Betta'lain sat between two bags of groceries on the backseat. Celery stood from one bag, a loaf of bread hung from the other, and in her lap Betta'lain held a bag of oranges.

"The way he's laying ain't natural."

"He was standing when we left." Betta'lain pointed. Her finger, pale as the celery, shook under the sleeve of her brown poodlecloth coat. She wore a purple beanie with an aluminum propeller on top. "Right there"—she said—"he was leaning over the fence like he wanted to say something. 'Bye, pony,' I said. 'Bye now.'"

Betta'lain pulled her beanie tighter. She wore it every waking minute, her short silver hair curling around it like moss.

"Right there." She made a smudge on the window with her finger. She made another smudge beside it, laughed, made a whole row, then another, until it looked like a school of minnows. "Hey, pony," she called, "bye, pony."

"If he's dead"—Leona stopped the car, reached inside the rusty mailbox twisted on its post as though somebody had tried to wring it off—"I'm not having it. Pearly Postom can pay what he owes just the same. Just the same."

She read her electric bill of $6.37 and crumpled a folder that said that "Little George," the famous midget singing cowboy minister, would lead a revival next week at the Big Oak Baptist in Luthersville. "Only four-feet-six and every ounce the gospel," the circular said.

"Anybody with a head as big as that"—Leona threw the folder into a kudzu-covered ditch—"can't be all there."

The pony still had not moved as she turned into the road and headed for the garage. He had belonged to the last family to live in the "old Tew Homeplace." It made Leona mad when anybody called it old. That place, she'd snort, is warm and tight and more than good enough for anybody who's ever rented it the last twenty-five years. Grandpa Tew built things to last and all the lumber was cut off this property and dried for two years before the house was built.

She pumped her brakes. Betta'lain bounced in the back seat, her mouth opening, closing like a puppet. "Stop."

"Stop," Leona told the car, and it did, two inches from the garage door.

Oranges spilled into Betta'lain's lap. She held one to the light, turned it around until she found the navel, and laughed. "There's nothing you can do about it," she said to the orange. "Nothing in this world. A dead pony can't be made alive."

"I most certainly can do something about it," Leona huffed. "If my foot didn't hurt, I'd had the sheriff after Postom long ago. Even if that pony is better off where he is now, dead, or in my pasture. He's got privileges here he wouldn't have in town. No big boys to ride him down . . . grass to eat."

Betta'lain peeled an orange, dropped each bit of skin out the window.

Leona tied a green scarf over her head. It had irregular polka dots on it and as many wrinkles as a paper hat. "Somebody in this family has got to see to that pony, even if it's somebody who's not able in the least."

"Nine, ten." Betta'lain dropped peels.

"Doctors don't operate on ingrown toenails every day of the week and say, 'Stay off your feet, Leona, take it easy, Leona.'" She looked at the bandaged swollen foot in the pink terrycloth slipper. "If I go getting this foot wet . . ." She buttoned her coat. "There's still dew in that tall grass . . ."

"It's after three." Betta'lain spit a seed, poked in another orange slice, and chewed. "I heard it on the drugstore news."

"Anybody who stands in a public place and watches demonstration television sets looks stupid. You ought to know better." Leona unlocked the car door. "Most people go about their business. The world doesn't always wait, you know."

The pony had not moved. "I can't believe he'd lay that way if something wasn't bad wrong."

"He was all right this morning." Betta'lain wiped sticky juice from her chin, licked her fingers. "I said, 'Bye, pony,' and he—"

"Don't you carry a handkerchief?" Leona snapped. "Mama always told me never to leave the house without one somewhere on me."

"She never told me," Leona said. "When she died, she didn't have as many lines as I got now." She handed Betta'lain a blue handkerchief with a tatted edge. "But then she didn't have you to look after all these years."

"What?" Betta'lain munched another orange slice.

"Don't eat so many you won't eat supper. You may have to be the one to cook it." Leona stepped from the car, held her foot carefully up. "Pony, honey," she called.

The animal didn't move. She couldn't tell if he was breathing or not; his rear and flanks looked bloated, swollen.

"If I take cold in this toe," she said to a dark cloud directly overhead, "I could die and then what would happen?"

Betta'lain pulled white membrane from the orange skin with her teeth; they protruded like a horse's. No manners, Leona thought, and no help. None whatsoever. Eat, eat, eat, and that pony out there dead or dying.

She hobbled to the gate and unlatched it. The gate was made from the iron frame of an old bed headboard some renter had left. Most of the time it was hire somebody to haul junk to the dump, but this time she got use from it. She'd showed Pearly Postom the picture of such a gate in the "Handy Helps" section of "Today's Farmer" and he'd made it.

She swung the gate shut. There was a lot you could do with things, if you took time. She didn't know about the pony. All he'd done so far was eat hay and run up her winter feed bill.

"I heard ponies are the worst thing there is on a pasture fence," she told Postom once.

"Naw," he said, rolling his wad of tobacco around stumpy yellow teeth. "Ain't no worse than nothing else."

"I heard if ponies aren't watched, they'll tear a fence down in no time."

"Little pony like he is"—Postom propped on his hoe handle in the cornfield—"why, a good puff of wind could push him over. He can't do a fence no damage."

Leona was not satisfied and watched her fence for signs. A month after Postom took his job working third shift at the mill, she made him move. How long he'd been working there before she found out, the Lord only knew, but Len Ralston let it slip one day in town. "That renter of yours is turning into a pretty good hand," he said. "Looks like it would kill him to move, but he gets his work done."

"What?" she said, and almost dropped her cup of Caroline's best Russian tea.

No wonder she hadn't been getting any work out of him. He was worn out from his mill job, sneaking off when she wasn't watching and coming home before she knew he'd been gone.

"You're doing more work for that mill than me," she told Postom, "so go live in one of their houses. See if they let you get behind in your rent."

The morning Postom and his boys packed stuff in some pickup truck they borrowed (it looked held together by baling wire), she stood on the porch and watched.

"We ain't got no place for the pony," he said. "Is it all right to leave him till we do?"

"You can leave that pony till you pay for what he ate of last winter's feed bill," she said.

Postom turned on his heel like a gear, got in the truck, and gunned it thundering and roaring down the hill. "He's doing that on purpose," she told Betta'lain. "Never had a lick of sense."

Betta'lain sat on the steps holding one of the multicolored cats that kept multiplying like mushrooms. Everywhere she looked, there was a new one. "I'd rather have somebody working this place that had some common sense than a person with all the degrees they give away at State College."

"Shoot," said Betta'lain, holding the cat's face to hers, "you never get neither."

Sometimes Leona was surprised at the clearness of Betta'lain's mind. She could be almost like a normal person, the things she came out with at times. Most days she trotted room-to-room wearing her beanie, carrying her wicker Easter egg basket. In the basket she had broken strings of beads, every Christmas card she or Mama ever received, valentines they'd made and never sent, some crochet hooks, half a box of raisins, and some nibbled cookies.

Leona didn't know how she'd manage—Betta'lain, the pony, her toe. She walked the path, dodged two greenish-black stacks of manure. "I wouldn't mind having a goat or two on the place, if it wasn't for the stink of them. At least they do their business neat and it don't pile up a pasture."

She held her bandaged foot away from the grass as much as possible, hobbled slowly. If the pony was to get up, she'd turn around and go back to the car this minute. Not waste her energies.

As she got closer, she saw gnats and bright green flies circling the pony in a haze.

The pony flicked an ear; or did she imagine it? The sun glared so. She cupped a hand over her eyes, plodded on.

She knew Betta'lain would have all the oranges peeled before she got back. I'll make ambrosia, she thought, I'll have to. Her feet hurt now, both of them.

The pony's eyes looked leaden. She heard a whinny of a rumble from his stomach, like he'd swallowed something alive. How long did stomachs live after an animal died?

"Lordy." Leona squatted over him. "You're not a bit dead. Fooling me all the time." She reached out to him and he flounced his head, neighed nasty teeth. His breath smelled like an old man's.

"Oh, oh . . ."

She stepped back too fast and felt moisture seep through her slipper and stain the bandage.

"Betta'lain," she hollered, hopping toward the car.

The pony rolled a few times, beat the ground with his limp mop of a tail and got to his feet. He hobbled a few steps like his feet hurt, all four of them.

"Pony"—as he came around beside her—"what happened to you?"

He pulled past her, limped toward the gate.

Betta'lain had the drive littered with peel. They can lay there till they rot for all I care, Leona decided. I don't have the strength to pick them up. Her toe ached like a decayed tooth and the smell of the slipper and bandage was making her head hurt.

"'Lain," she called at the gate, "somebody's hurt the pony."

Betta'lain had all the peeled oranges back in the sack. She carried them dripping from the car. "I saw him," she said.

"Who? Saw who?"

"Him that had the pony before us."

"Postom?" Leona followed Betta'lain toward the house. "What are you talking about?"

"He was behind the barn all the time. Didn't you see?"
Betta'lain waited for Leona to open the door. "Him and the biggest boy. They had a rope."

"He was trying to take him without paying me," Leona screamed at the barn, shook her fist. "The only pay I get from his bills, three months back bills, and here he comes stealing it away. Tried to ride the pony off and it couldn't hold their weight, that's what."

"He left," Betta'lain said.

Leona looked toward the bent pony by the gate. "Any man with common sense would have known to lead him off, not try to ride a little thing like that."

She sat on the steps, watched the sun that lay like a spent gold piece. Her toe hurt, throbbed like a pump that drained everything in her out.

She could hear Betta'lain singing in the kitchen. "I'm a little teapot, short and stout, tip me over, pour me out."

"I'm poured out," Leona said. "That Postom—there's not a drop of me left."

The pony whinkered at her, turned and stumbled toward the pond.

Leona blinked in the kitchen light. Betta'lain had set the table, two spoons on each of the four "Our State Bird" plastic placemats. The bald oranges were stacked in a pryamid in a bowl.

Leona took her seat and Betta'lain tied a chain of tea bags around her neck. She wore an identical one. "Sing." Betta'lain waved a wooden spoon. "I'm a little . . ."

"If I had a gun"—Leona stirred her tea—"I'd shoot him."

Pieces of Crow

THE SCRAPS OF yellow taffeta lay on the floor like shattered sunshine. I held Joey, warm from his nap, clean in a freshly ironed sunsuit. Keeping him quiet while Daddy slept and Mama sewed was my job. It wasn't always this easy.

Mama knelt at the stool where Nina Baldridge stood turning like the ballerina on my music box. I hummed "Sweetheart Waltz" for Joey. He laughed, reached for the sun spangles in the air.

"Am I pinning this too short?" Mama stood, brushed back her hair. The pincushion on her waist looked like a nest of spiders, all with silver legs.

Mrs. Baldridge, feet fat in black lace-up shoes, sat with her ankles crossed. She wore a veiled hat and under the net her face was damp as though a mist rained on her.

"We can make the dress longer if you like. I have plenty of material for the hem." Mama stood back from the fidgeting Nina.

Mrs. Baldridge walked around, ducking, unducking her head like a chicken. I could almost hear her cluck.

"It's about an eighth-inch shorter over here." Mrs. Baldridge pinched the air as if she were making a bird's beak.

Joey clapped his hands for her to do it again.

"Cute." She patted him on the head. A minister's wife had to go around doing things like that.

"I check it all the way around before I hem," Mama said. "Right now we're more interested in the right length." She helped Nina step from the stool, the long yellow gown swishing like a curtain. Nina was fourteen, two years older than I was, secretary of the student council, a cheerleader, and one of the most popular girls in school. "We don't want the dress so long you trip over it," Mama said.

"I'd die if I tripped." Nina made a face under her thick makeup mask. Pimples made her cheeks rough as an orange. She also had pimples on her back. "If I fell"—Nina slid into high-heeled pumps—"Susie would say I did it on purpose to ruin her wedding."

"Your sister would not say anything of the sort," Mrs. Baldridge said. "Nina, what makes you say such things?"

Nina stuck her tongue out. I giggled. Mrs. Baldridge was behind her adjusting the back of her dress. "I still think it's cut too low, neck and back."

Mama had shaped darts so Nina could wear a padded bra. She looked nice.

"I don't see why Nina thinks she's supposed to have as much up there as Susie's friends," Mrs. Baldridge said. "They're all college girls."

I rocked Joey. Nina, as she paraded by, said, "He's cute." I wondered if she planned to marry a minister when she grew up and was practicing. Since Mama had been sewing this bridesmaid's dress, Nina said "hi" to me in the hall at school. I always said "hi" back.

This was the first dress Mama made for anyone for pay. She made my clothes, hers, some for Joey, and several things for women in the neighborhood, but she never charged them—they were neighbors. They were the ones who told her to start sewing for the public. That's when Mama ran the ad in the paper and Mrs. Baldridge answered.

"Taffeta has to be one of the hardest things in the world to sew," Mama said after they left. "And a bridesmaid's dress—I've never made one before. I'll be glad when it's finished and I get paid. I'll have earned every cent of it."

Mama was trying to earn some extra money. School would open in three weeks and all my dresses were too short. Joey needed winter things, Daddy a jacket—so many things, Mama said.

"You must think you're going to get rich," Daddy said at the table. He worked at the all-night gas station, his first job in four months. It was late afternoon and he looked sleepy, tired. "It's not that easy, nothing is." When he lost his job at Coleman's after ten years, Mama said it hurt him more than anyone knew.

"Every little bit helps," she said, putting beans on to cook. "It costs so much these days to live."

Daddy drank coffee. His eyes seemed as deep as cups.

Mama's second customer was a Mrs. Lanning who had a crippled daughter my age. "She's been in a wheelchair all her life," Mama said when she hung up the phone. "Poor thing." She looked at me for a moment, then hugged hard. "Sometimes I forget how lucky we really are."

The afternoon the Lannings came, I waited by the window. Mama told me to meet them at the car and help Cloene, the crippled girl, be nice to her, play dolls or games if she could from her wheelchair.

A Buick, big, black as a whale, stopped in the drive. It crunched gravels like they were being swallowed. I ran to the car and saw myself in the shiny hubcaps, all moon-faced and fish-eyed, as I waited for them to get out.

Cloene lay against the seat, eyes closed as if asleep. Her mouth jerked open once and I saw teeth too large and crowded for one person.

Mrs. Lanning came around the car, yanked off leather gloves like she was mad at them. She opened the door so fast I was pushed into a prickle bush. "I been doing this so long, nobody but me knows how." She handed me her purse and gloves to hold. A scalloped handkerchief was caught in her purse and flowered out like a purple blossom.

"When Cloene falls," Mrs. Lanning said, "she goes sprawling and there's nothing you can do but get out of her way."

I saw rubber-tipped crutches step to the ground, then one leg in a heavy brown shoe, then another. Both were held in cages of silver braces.

"Look out," Mrs. Lanning called, helping the huddle of shiny bones toward the house. "Look now."

Cloene thrashed and flailed metal. Deep cries choked in her throat.

"No." Mrs. Lanning pulled at her. "No, we're not going back in the car. No." She turned to me. "Cloene would ride twenty-four hours a day. Sometimes when I can't do anything with her, we get in the car and ride. But with the price of gas these days . . ."

Mrs. Lanning pushed Cloene into a porch chair, took her purse and gloves, pulled out the handkerchief, and wiped and fanned herself. "I don't know why I pick the hottest day of the year to do things."

Cloene lay to one side of the chair as though she'd been tossed there. Black curls that looked carved clung to her head and the dress she wore was a faded green thing, zippered like a sack. One sleeve had a tear. She kept kicking her feet, made clanking noises on the porch.

"No,"—Mrs. Lanning slapped her leg—"we are not going. You calm yourself down and sit still."

Mama came then. "Bethann, get one of your dolls or something for Cloene to play with."

I ran for Rosalie on my bed. Grandma had mailed me Rosalie for Christmas. She was my favorite and best. She had pigtails, her own straw hat, patent shoes with buttons no bigger than a bug's eye. Mama had made her polka-dot dress with tucks, scraps of lace, and a ruffle.

"Cloene looks about the same size as Bethann," Mama said.

"We can measure and find out. If she is, I'll be glad to use some of Bethann's patterns and save you buying some."

Cloene stared straight ahead, one foot tapped the floor. Her hands lay like dead fish in her lap. I gently gave her Rosalie.

She screamed and swept my doll to the floor in a clatter. I grabbed poor Rosalie. Her hand was broken off. I held it, almost crying. "Mama, look."

"We'll glue it back, honey," she said. "Go put Rosalie away. One of your old cloth dolls might have been better."

I kissed Rosalie, held her hollow stump like I wanted to hide it.

"I'm sure Cloene didn't mean it," Mama said.

"Yes, she did." Mrs. Lanning spanked Cloene's arm. "Bad girl. Bad."

When I came back from bandaging Rosalie's arm, Mama and Mrs. Lanning had black material spread across their laps, the chairs, and spilling onto the floor. If you looked at the cloth closely enough you could see tiny blue dots, but the rest of it was black as thunder. "Ugh," I said.

Mama gave me a look that said don't say anything else. Her eyes added, *please.* "Don't you think a brighter color would be better for Cloene? Little girls like—"

"I know what little girls like," Mrs. Lanning said. "But Cloene isn't any little girl. If she weren't my sister's child, I wouldn't be doing all I do for her."

"She isn't your daughter?" Mama smoothed the fabric. A large wrinkle had been folded in the center.

"Not for a minute," Mrs. Lanning said, "even if we have had the responsibility for her since she was a month old. Elsie died and we were the only ones to take the baby. That's before we knew she was so . . . damaged."

Poor Cloene. No mother and having to wear black dresses.

"I think there's enough material here to make her five dresses." Mrs. Lanning folded the fabric.

"Five?" Mama said. "Alike? Don't you think she'll get tired of—"

"It doesn't matter." Mrs. Lanning waved her hand. "Cloene never notices what she wears and what she doesn't."

I couldn't watch Mama and Mrs. Lanning as they tried to take Cloene's measurements. I heard from inside the house. Mama tried to soothe her, show her the tape measure wouldn't hurt. Mrs. Lanning shouted and pulled her around. The chair scraped.

"Now do you see why I can't take her into a store and buy a dress? She fights me every step of the way."

Mama helped Cloene to the car and Mrs. Lanning said she appreciated what Mama was going to do. She said she had tried to order things for Cloene by mail and never got what she wanted. "They send you the worst stuff they have just to see if you'll keep it," Mrs. Lanning said.

The car sped off in a loud blast. Mama folded the awful material and took it in the house.

When she cut out the dresses the next day, the black material fell to the floor like dead birds. Pieces of crow. Mama told me to get out her remnant box and look for any scraps of blue. She would use them for pockets or collars or trim, any way she could to dress up that deathly black. "Did you notice what beautiful blue eyes Cloene had?" Mama asked.

At the fabric shop Mama bought lace. "It won't take much for a collar," she said, "and all little girls should wear some lace once in a while." Before we left the store we looked again at the material we wanted for my school dresses. I held the red and yellow plaid out from the bolt, rubbed the green cotton with its red apple design. "Mrs. Lanning should buy material like these for Cloene," Mama said. "A pity. She bought good material, paid a lot for it, but what a color."

At night Mama hemmed near the lamp. The yellow taffeta talked as it slid through her fingers. Poured like a waterfall off her lap as she worked. She couldn't sew on Cloene's dresses at night.

On Friday when the Baldridges picked up Nina's dress,

Mama had it pressed and floating on a hanger. They examined the seams and sleeves, said she had done a fine job, and paid her nine dollars. She put the money in the top drawer of the sewing machine.

I built blocks with Joey on the cool linoleum floor. All the colors were gone. Mama had mopped and scrubbed and swept them away.

At the sewing machine she finished Cloene's dresses. She had used scraps to make sashes and pockets on some, round as muffins. Another had buttons in a row on the yoke. Each dress was different and Mama was pleased. She pressed and hung them around the room.

Mrs. Lanning hurried in, left the motor running in the car. When she saw the dresses she drew up her face, took a breath big enough to blow the house down. "You mean you made all five dresses like this?" She snatched at the first one.

"I tried to make them as different as possible from the same material," Mama said.

"They're not what I had in mind at all." Mrs. Lanning threw a dress on the bed. "They're not practical. She'll only get a collar dirty, tear off a pocket. Lace is a waste of time. She doesn't know the difference." Mrs. Lanning threw three other dresses down. "They simply won't do."

"I'm sorry," Mama said. "I didn't think you'd mind if I tried to make them as attractive as possible. The material was so drab, depressing. It needed—"

"You've ruined my material." Mrs. Lanning's face was red. "I'll have to start over."

"I don't understand," Mama said. She put the dresses back on hangers. "You don't want the dresses. I don't know what to do."

"I don't care what you do with them." Mrs. Lanning spun around. "That's your problem. But I do expect reimbursement for my material. It's ruined as far as I am concerned."

"I didn't ruin it," Mama said. "I've never had anyone who didn't like my work. I double-stitch seams, sew buttons by hand—people say they're better than ready-made."

"I expect replacement for my material," Mrs. Lanning said. She patted her purse. "Five dollars at least."

"What about—"

"The fabric cost more than that, of course," Mrs. Lanning said. "But five would be fair."

I thought of the money in the sewing machine drawer. "Don't," I said under my breath. "Don't."

"My time is worth something," Mama said.

"I'm in a hurry." Mrs. Lanning stood at the door. "This did not turn out like I had hoped. A matter of communication. I should have known." She gazed around the room.

Mama took the money from the drawer, counted out five ones.

I felt sick. In the other bedroom, Joey started to fuss. He would wake Daddy.

Mrs. Lanning shoved the money in her purse, snapped it shut, and walked out.

For a minute Mama didn't move. Then she put the rest of the money back, got up, and closed the machine.

"It's not fair." I ran to her. "You worked hard and the dresses were nice."

"I know." She touched one.

I took a dress and held it before me. "Will I have to wear them now?"

"They would fit, wouldn't they?" Mama said.

Joey yelled from his crib. He wanted up.

I thought of the plaid I wanted, the pretty dresses Mama and I planned.

"No." Mama took the dress. "You won't have to wear them. I'll give them to the Clothing Closet or somebody, but you don't have to wear them." She put her arm around me. "We're not that poor. Not now, not ever."

Green Lightning and the Tablecloth Bride

TALK ABOUT FAST weddings. I think my mother and Aunt Harriet once set some kind of record. In less than three hours they had the wedding dress, bride's bouquet, cake (complete with wedded couple), a borrowed piano, and Uncle Elmo in his stocking feet, playing "The Yellow Rose of Texas."

It happened the summer I was twelve. The longest, hottest, driest summer anyone had ever seen. Green skies boiled daily, cooked with lightning, burned black, and ended up spitting a few hot drops that plopped hard as marbles in the dust.

Neighbors sat on porches and fanned with cardboard fans labeled, "We Are Your Friend in Time of Need," compliments of Herman's Funeral Home. Aunt Harriet had a painted, folded Japanese fan with a pink tassel. The tassel flicked around her wrist like a fly as she fanned. She kept the fan in a tall crystal vase on the piano in her dark and mothball-smelling living room. "Go get me my fan, May Kay," Aunt Harriet sat on our porch and sang. Mama added, "Run, honey." And gave me a look. I ran across the street, got the fan but not before I tried it out a few times posing in the long mirror above the piano. I fanned, tried to make my eyes look slanted. They never did. Nothing I did worked out right that summer. I was too big and awkward to take turns with the kids playing with the hose or jumping through yard sprinklers. The pool in the backyard was for little kids like my brother Lester. "Baby Squirt," I called him when Mama couldn't hear. Everybody I knew had gone to the beach or mountains for the summer. It was awful. I read a lot, walked downtown to the library and carried home armloads of books. When I wasn't reading, I pretended to be. Held a book in front of my face and listened for all I was worth. Everybody forgot I was there.

Twelve was bad, but being the only girl in the neighborhood was worse. Except I wasn't really the only girl. There was Frances Anne Gurley on the corner, but she was twenty-one and treated me the way I treated the rest of the kids. Like I was the lowest kind of brat. Frankie dated Shorty Privette every Sunday, Tuesday, and Thursday night. For their thirteenth month going-together-anniversary, Shorty gave her a fuzzy black ball of a dog named Mop and took her to the Riverview Fish Camp where you get all you can eat for two dollars.

One of the differences between this summer and last, was that on Monday, Wednesday, and Friday nights Frankie's new boyfriend, Leon Futty, came to see her. Saturday nights she stayed home.

"What for?" my father once asked.

"A girl has to catch her breath once in a while," Mama said, "and wash her hair."

"Oh." Daddy went back to his VFW magazine with the jumping deer and bow and arrow on the cover.

Mother gave him a look to freeze any deer in midleap.

Saturday nights Frankie did wash her hair and do her

nails. She held her fingers wide apart, waved them in the air like a handful of matches. She sat in her green and white gingham robe with cherries embroidered on the pockets, her feet tucked under and hidden in a fat, red velvet chair. Mop curled on her lap and we watched the Texaco Hour with Milton Berle, Beat the Clock with Bud Cox, and Your Hit Parade with Snooky Lanson and Dorothy Collins.

"Don't Bud Cox look just like Shorty?" she said once. "With that high forehead and all?"

I didn't know. We watched everything that moved on the television, even the test pattern, which didn't move and which Frankie said looked like the Indian on the nickel, only bigger.

Frankie's mother, Sudie Gurley, knitted while we watched. Her needles clicked and scraped like grasshoppers, a dry sound like the one Frankie made scraping off three coats of nail polish in chips and peels.

"Why don't you use remover?" Sudie asked. "It wouldn't be half the mess."

"Because I can't stand the smell." Frankie stuck out her tongue. I giggled.

"Anybody who can stand doggy breath . . ." Sudie's needles snapped faster. "It can't be good for you to sleep with that dog every night."

"It's my room"—Frankie wrinkled her nose—"and I'll sleep with whoever I want to."

The way she talked to her mother made me feel tough inside, and I kept a file of things to say when I got her age. I doubted I'd ever get around to it, though.

Frankie's room had been added onto the duplex where the Gurleys lived, five years ago. One time her father came home from wherever he stayed, started the room, got it framed in, roofed, and floored, then was suddenly called away on business, or so Sudie told Mama.

"Poker game," Aunt Harriet said. "Monkey business." She also told Mama that Ed Baynes, who owned the duplex, told her one day he drove up to collect the rent and there was a man on the roof tacking shingles. He never said a word, just lifted his hat and kept tacking. Sudie counted out the rent and didn't mention it. Ed said Sudie always paid her rent on time and she had for the last twenty years and he didn't want to ask questions that might embarrass her or cause hard feelings. So Ed paid for the rest of the room to be finished and felt it was a good investment, even if he hadn't thought of it himself.

Grover Gurley was in and out, mostly out, most of the year. He came home for Christmas, the Fourth of July, a few times in between. He sent money every month though. "At least they aren't living off the county," Aunt Harriet said whenever anyone snipped or gossiped about Sudie or Frankie.

All Sudie Gurley ever said was, "May Kay, don't you marry a gambling man. He'll write you fancy letters, then walk off and you'll never know when, or if, you'll ever see him again." She showed me a packet of dusty-looking letters tied together with a bluish-green ribbon. "Isn't that the most beautiful handwriting you've ever seen for a man?" She traced the curls of her name in the crinkle of brown ink.

Mama and Aunt Harriet wondered what her choice was in Frankie's boyfriends. She told them Shorty was as steady a boy as you'd ever want. Not a minute late, never a second too early, and he always had Frances Anne home on the very tick of twelve. And Shorty's gifts to her, other than Mop, which she was sure was Frances Anne's idea, also pleased her. A Blue Waltz perfume set—the big one with bathpowder, spray, and twelve-ounce perfume. For her birthday a watch, and at Christmas a toaster. On Valentine's Day he had given her a diamond. You had to squint to see it, but if Frankie held her hand out and at an angle to the light, and you looked really hard, you could see a tiny glint. Sudie said his car was paid for and he had eight hundred dollars in the bank. When he dated Frankie, he wore green pants with a sharp crease and his hair was wet combed, so wavy it made you dizzy to look long. He was smart, Sudie told Mama and

Aunt Harriet. He drove a Pepsi truck and had taught himself to play the guitar in twelve easy lessons.

Leon, Frankie's new boyfriend, or Number Two as Daddy called him, was a preacher's son. He brought his daddy's old pulpit Bible once to show Sudie and Frankie, led them in a devotion. "That boy"—Sudie wiped her glasses—"can pray the prettiest prayer. It will tear your heart right out." She said she wouldn't be a bit surprised if Leon didn't get the Call any day to go preach.

Daddy laughed, hooted out loud and slapped his knees when he heard that. "Anybody who calls that boy deserves him," he said. "Ha . . . haw. That's a good one."

Leon's last job had been in the poultry plant and he said he'd die if he ever so much as had to look at another chicken in any shape or form.

"That ought to be proof right there," Daddy laughed. "If he don't eat chicken, he'll never be a preacher."

After the chicken job folded, Leon didn't seem in a hurry to find anything else. Daddy worked him one day at the hardware. "He couldn't count nails," I heard him tell Mama. "Lester can do that and he's just a kid. Nails," Daddy groaned. Mama and Aunt Harriet didn't say anything after that. Daddy had tried. He had given the boy a chance and if he didn't choose to take it, whose fault was it. They looked to Uncle Elmo, who ran a plumbing business. "Not for a minute," he said. "You gotta know what you're doing when you mess around people's pipes. I'm not taking a chance."

Leon didn't own a car and walked nine miles to eat supper with Sudie and Frankie on his date nights. Then he and Frankie sat on Gurley's stoop and batted bugs that sizzled and hit the light. Or they'd walk around the block, go downtown to a movie or the drugstore. Several neighbors said Leon sure didn't look like any preacher's son they'd ever seen and he walked like he didn't have enough sense to put one foot in front of the other.

Mama said it was wonderful Frances Anne had two calling on her and she could make a choice.

"Some choice," Aunt Harriet sighed behind her fan.

Everyone waited for the day Shorty and Leon would meet, either by accident or plan. "After all," Mama said, "she is engaged to one of them." I wondered if it would be pistols or swords for Frankie's flame-nail-polished and fat-fingered white hand. Fists or duel at dawn? Mama said I'd been reading too many old romance books and she didn't know where I got that kind of thing. Maybe I was in the section I wasn't suppposed to go in the library. "Children's is on the right, May Kay," she told me, "the right side." I had been slipping through for years and Miss Laura Kelsey just stamped out my books and didn't bother to read titles and authors anymore.

I wanted them to duel. That would be exciting.

"Those two—" Daddy said, one night after Leon walked past, "when he and Shorty do meet—they'll probably take one look at each other and *run*."

I frowned at him. What an awful thing to say.

"Hush," Mama said. "Somebody might hear you."

If Sudie worried about her daughter's decision, she didn't show it. France Anne dated during the week, watched TV on Saturdays, and kept saying Shorty sure did look a lot like Bud Cox. Same handsome high forehead.

"A sure sign of intelligence." Sudie counted stitches in the sweater she knitted. "My daddy had a high forehead and he served as Court Solicitor for Harnet County four terms in a row."

"Leon's got the prettiest eyes." Frankie reached between her legs, lifted up Mop, held him high in the air, and blew fluff off her face. Mop swam in the air, snapped small, pointed teeth.

I told Mama about the business of high foreheads meaning a lot of intelligence. She canned peaches, pushing them in jars with the back of the spoon. "Don't bet on it," she said.

"Is that so?" Daddy walked into the kitchen, took half a peeled peach and bit into it. "All the time I thought Frankie loved Shorty for his musical abilities."

When Shorty drove his Pepsi truck down Woodward Street twice a day, he played "Shave and a Haircut" on the horn.

"Thank God for Saturdays and Sundays," Mama said. "Sometimes I hear that tune in my sleep."

Shorty also played the guitar, picked and pulled it more than singing with it. Sometimes he sat on the stoop with Frankie for hours. Frankie in a blue dotted-swiss dress that took Sudie four hours of hard ironing, fanned out like a lake around her. Frankie, blue satin bow in her curls round as radishes, crossed her ankles in their white socks, patted her sandaled feet and listened, her face upturned as a bird.

Leon didn't look like he could lift a guitar without getting a hernia. But he could hold more lightning bugs in his hands at one time than anyone I'd ever seen.

We counted 206 once until Frankie started goosing him under his arms and he got so tickled he let go. That was when Mama called me in.

"It's not late," I fussed, "and you can't say tomorrow is a school day because it's not." School wouldn't start for two weeks yet and I both wanted it and yet dreaded for the summer to end.

"I know when it's time for you to come home," Mama said and shut her mouth before anything else came out.

A week before school started, the last of the hottest August on record in forty years of weather-keeping, Frankie made her choice. She gave Shorty back his diamond, the toaster, what was left of the Blue Waltz perfume set, and kept Mop. Sudie walked the street telling first one neighbor, then another, how "that boy actually broke down and cried." She twisted an embroidered handkerchief when she said it. "Frances Anne broke his heart plain and simple. I told her," Sudie went on, "that whatever became of him now would always be on her head. That boy came up and hugged me, said he'd always love me and a real mother couldn't have treated him any better. I cried, he cried some more. We had us a crying good time."

When Sudie was telling Mama, I wondered what Frankie was doing while all this crying was going on. She was probably watching "As the World Turns" and not hearing a thing being said.

"When are Frances Anne and Leon planning to get married?" Mama asked.

"Why, right now," Sudie said. "The sooner the better, that's what she said. When Frances Anne wants to do a thing, she won't wait. Once she makes up her mind, you have to—"

"Now?" Mama's jaw dropped low enough to spring a hinge. (That's what Daddy always said she did.) "Now?" Mama said again.

"Well, today." Sudie looked at the little gold biscuit of a watch she wore on a neck chain. Her grandmother's watch. One of the few things she ever got from her family. "They never accepted my marriage," she said once, "never forgave me."

"But it's Wednesday," Mama said. "Nobody gets married on *Wednesday*. Besides, the stores are closed this afternoon."

"That's what I said." Sudie snapped her watch shut. "But you know Frances Anne when she makes her mind up."

"Can't she wait until Saturday?"

"Leon's gone home to tell his daddy, change clothes, and get his things now," Sudie said.

As soon as Sudie left, Mama stopped peeling apples for supper and dashed for the phone. She came back to the kitchen a minute later, sat down and sighed. "There's not a preacher in this town. I don't know what we'd do if somebody decided to die."

Aunt Harriet slipped in the back door. "I know it and as I walked across the street, I remembered old Mr. Ledbetter— over on Hathaway. He's retired, but that won't make any difference."

"He's deaf!" Mama peeled and quartered an apple.

"If he can say the words and sign his name, it ought to do

the trick," Aunt Harriet said, and picked up an apple.

Mama went to the phone in the hall, came back in a few minutes waving her arms. "Victory," she said. "He'll do it, but not until after three o'clock. That's his rug-hooking time and his nap."

"May Kay." Mama looked at me. I'd just taken an apple, was open to bite. "Go tell Sudie it's three o'clock and we'll do the best we can with what we got."

"What about her dress?" Aunt Harriet spun a red peeling around in her hands, the apple balding with each stroke.

"Sudie says they've got her white organdy graduation dress and Frankie was freshening it up with some spray starch."

"And I've got a new lace cloth for that little round table in the front bedroom." Aunt Harriet took another apple. "She could wear that for a veil, even if it is heavy. It's never been used."

I ducked out the door and across the street so fast the hot tar didn't burn my bare feet. Frankie was not ironing her dress after all. She was deep in the dark corners of her room behind towering columns of magazines, *True Heart* and *Intimate Romances*. "Don't you ever let your Mama know I give you those," she said as I left with my arms loaded. "She might think the wrong thing."

Aunt Harriet had sent all the kids in the neighborhood out to pick Queen Anne's lace and "anything white that's blooming." "All I got is red geraniums," she said, "and orange gladiolias—and we sure don't want those."

I couldn't see why not. Red was a pretty color. So was orange. White was no color at all.

Lester and I were sent uptown to the Martin Sisters' Sweet Shoppe. "Hurry," Mama said, and pushed twenty dollars in my hand. "Take any kind of white cake they got—round or square or sheet—and decorated—as long as it doesn't say Happy Birthday or Bon Voyage—just plain cake."

We had to wait for the train to pass. It had seventy-seven cars and I won because I'd guessed seventy-two. Lester punched me in the arm and I ran after him as he whizzed around the corner. The Sweet Shoppe was closed and there was nothing in the window but a few scattered cupcakes with clowns on them and a sign saying, "Fishing." A station wagon disappeared down the street with two white heads bobbing and a bunch of fishing poles waving their corks like a game at the county fair.

"Fools," Aunt Harriet said. "Don't they know it's too hot for fish to bite on a day like this? Fish got more sense than some people."

Mama said that was what she was afraid might happen and she'd whipped up a mix cake. "We'll put white icing on it and call it cake," she said, dumping powdered sugar in a bowl. It swirled up a sweet-smelling cloud. Lester went across the street to get the little bride and groom dolls that were from the fiftieth wedding anniversary cake Aunt Harriet and Uncle Elmo had in June. Aunt Harriet cut the gold foil "50" from behind them and said, "Now . . . that's the same thing, isn't it?"

I planned to loan my bride and groom paperdolls from last year when I played junk like that, but I was glad I didn't have to. They'd get icing on them and I might play with them again when nobody would know.

"Girls don't get married but once—or shouldn't," Aunt Harriet said. "And at least the first time ought to be a little special." Aunt Harriet stood back from the cake. She had made marshmallow flowers and put white borders with a tube Mama used for our birthday cakes. On a lace doily and milkglass stand, the cake looked pretty after all. "You never know what you can do until you try." Aunt Harriet wiped sugar from her fingers.

"It does look better I thought." Mama gave me and Lester the bowls to lick.

"It will have to do," Harriet sighed. "In the time we've had, I think we've done well."

My father came home at one. Mama met him at the door and backed him out. "Don't take your hat off," she said.

"Frances Anne is getting married and we have to move the piano."

"Whoa," Daddy said. He held his hat, had it ready to sail across to rest on the radio. "Not me," he said. "You all can just get Frances Anne married all you want to, but leave me out." All he wanted was a hot lunch and a cool nap in the swing under the fan.

"It can't take more than five minutes," Mama said, "and it's all downhill." She had a hand on his back, pushed. "We can't have a wedding without music."

"It's a hell of a lot of work to move a piano," Daddy said. "I'll sing."

"Lord." Mama raised both hands in the air. *That* would be all we'd need."

"It's the mountain to Mohammed." Daddy rubbed his hands together. "I hope Elmo's hernia's in shape for this." He hitched up his pants, followed Mama out the door, humming "Home on the Range."

After they pulled the piano from the wall, Aunt Harriet made everyone wait while she cleaned behind it. Christmas cards, church bulletins, her crocheted pineapple doily. "I wondered where that thing went." She shook lint tags off.

"I thought the cat ate it," Elmo chuckled.

"You accused Amy Rothwell of taking it after you had the circle meeting here last Easter." Mama cupped her hands over her mouth.

"Well, she always said she wanted it." Aunt Harriet bent to pick up marbles, pieces of chalk, crayons, bobbie pins, and an old key. Lester took the key, put it in his pocket, and grinned. "It's a skeleton key. I can get in every house on this street any time I want!"

"I'm as good a housekeeper as the next, and better than some, but pianos don't get moved every day of the week." Aunt Harriet swept.

"Thank God." Daddy wiped his forehead.

The vacuum cleaner salesman who appeared at the door was invited in. His eyes lit up at Aunt Harriet with the broom, sweeping the corner. "I got a tool that gets to places like that."

Lester and I carried the piano bench. It was full of sheet music that kept slipping and fluttering into the ditch. We finally had to park it on the lawn and take some out. We left it under the magnolia tree with a rock on top to keep it from blowing.

The men had the piano tilted on the steps like a sailboat about to be launched. "Hold her steady there, Revco," the vacuum cleaner saleman said.

"Elmo," my father said.

"If he does make a sale after this," Mama said, "you can't say he didn't earn every cent of it."

The piano rolled on the walk smoothly, old wheels squealing like cats fighting over a fence. As they turned the piano into the street, Sarah, Aunt Harriet's black and white tabby cat, strolled by and was nearly hit. Uncle Elmo said something I couldn't quite hear. Aunt Harriet frowned, said, "Hush." Mama, who followed along behind with a dustcloth and furniture polish, said, "Wouldn't that look good in the *News and Enquirer*? Cat Killed By Piano on Woodhaven Street."

"Wouldn't be half as dumb as most of the stuff they print," Uncle Elmo grunted.

"Pictures." Mama's hand flew to her cheek. "We haven't called someone to take pictures."

"Lester's got a camera," I said.

"I'll take the pictures," Daddy said. "I want to be standing behind something while all this is going on, even it it's nothing but a camera."

The piano moaned and leaned as the three men carried it across the yard to the empty apartment next to where Sudie and Frances Anne lived. It was Mama and Aunt Harriet's idea again. "Why not?" they said. The apartment had been freshly painted, floors refinished, windows scraped and washed. "It's clean as a church," they said. Ed Baynes said sure, it was fine by him to use it, just save him a piece of cake and cup of punch. He'd try to get by.

"I tell you," Daddy said after they rolled the piano to the corner of the living room, all the squeaks chasing around the empty room like ghosts. "Never again. Not for any man's money will I ever move that piano."

Uncle Elmo sat down and began "Chopsticks" and a rollicking version of "The Yellow Rose of Texas." "How's that for bridal music?" he asked.

"Not much," Aunt Harriet said. "I know you. You'll scandalize us."

She and Mama set up folding tables, covered them with sheets. "Blue candles were all I had—and the stores closed. What does Frances Anne think you can do on Wednesdays with the stores closing at noon and no notice."

"It looks just lovely." Mama stood back, hands on her hips. She had arranged Queen Anne's lace in a white basket and sent Lester back out to see if he couldn't find some kind of blue flowers growing somewhere, "to add some color."

Grandmother's carnival glass punch bowl was in the table's center. "Thank goodness Mama had the good taste to have the blue kind and not that horrible red-orange stuff." Aunt Harriet slid the bowl an inch to the right.

Sudie came flying in, waving her hands as if she were erasing something. "Her dress won't button. It's too tight. There's a gap at the top this big." She measured air with her fingers.

"I'll fix it." Aunt Harriet left. Mama always said Harriet was so good with a thread and needle she could outwit a spider if it came to it.

"What if you're going to all this trouble for nothing?" Uncle Elmo said. He took a handful of mints from the bag Mama opened. Aunt Harriet found them in back of the freezer left over from her anniversary party. "What if Frances Anne backs out? What if Leon decides not to show up? What if—?"

"The sky fell?" Daddy said as he went out the door. "My wife and your wife would pitch in start sweeping up the pieces and never look to see what happened or where it came from until after they finished."

Daddy dressed and fussed. He refused to wear a suit on his one afternoon a week off. "A sports shirt will do," Mama said, "if you'll wear a tie." Daddy sighed wetly.

She made me wear my yellow Easter dress, even though it was so tight I could hardly breathe and too short by three inches. "We're going to do our best for Frances Anne." She tugged on my skirt. "Nobody can say we didn't."

I wore white sandals and socks, my ankle bracelet with the one blank heart. I was waiting for the *right* initial to scratch on the other. I carried my gloves and the white Bible I got when I passed the Catechism at church.

Preacher Ledbetter was there in polka-dotted stockings. A bee stung his ankle as he walked across the grass. His foot swelled so, Mrs. Ledbetter had to go home for his carpet slippers.

Uncle Elmo was on the second round of "Here Comes the Bride" when Frances Anne came in the front door. Leon came in the back. He said there was such a crowd at the front, he couldn't get in. He wore a shiny blue suit with red striped tie and white shirt. His hair looked dark and wet combed back from his face. His forehead was pale as the underside of a melon.

Preacher Ledbetter cleared his throat and began, "We are gathered here today . . ." His voice ground like the motor on Lester's rock polisher.

At the end, Leon took a small jewelry box from his pocket, picked something from the blue velvet lips, and slid it on Frances Anne's finger. Then he kissed her so hard the veil slid off. Aunt Harriet dashed to catch it before it hit the floor, then shook and brushed it as though it had. I'd never be able to look at the tablecloth again without somehow seeing Frances Anne's face under it.

Uncle Elmo let roll with "The Beer Barrel Polka" and then Sudie danced with Preacher Ledbetter until her face was the color of Daddy's tie and she was making little gasps with her breath, laughing and hiccuping in between. Daddy swung me around a few times and Lester danced with Aunt Harriet who said thank goodness all this was taking place during the day or we'd be arrested for disturbing the peace.

"Who's to complain?" Daddy wiped his face. "We're all here." He had bubbled a quart of Uncle Elmo's homemade wild cherry wine in the punch bowl when Aunt Harriet wasn't looking. Aunt Harriet, cup in hand, said to Emmie Lou Ledbetter, the preacher's wife, that somebody, she wasn't saying who, sure didn't know how to brew tea for a punch so that you had a tea taste, yet wasn't too strong and bitter. She looked at Mama when she said it and I almost let the secret out by giggling. Then Aunt Harriet and Emmie Lou talked of ways you can brew tea to keep it from clouding.

The wedding cake was chocolate inside. Mama said that was the only mix she had in the house. Frances Anne said it was her favorite and how did Mama know? She cut the first piece and fed it so fast to Leon his cheeks bulged like a chipmunk and he had to put his hand up for her to stop. That was when Daddy snapped his picture. The flash froze everybody either bug-eyed or chewing.

Outside, kids came from six blocks away and stood in line for cake and punch.

"I never thought we'd have this many," Mama said and glanced at Lester. "It wasn't up to you to invite everybody you knew." She cut smaller pieces of cake. Aunt Harriet ladled out half-glasses of punch until the bowl was empty. They sent me home for Kool Aid and frozen lemonade. Daddy and Uncle Elmo said that was the worst-tasting stuff that ever got caught in a cup and traded glasses with the kids that got punch before the punch ran out.

Frances Anne left to change clothes to "go away" and Mama sent Leon to pick up all the plastic cups scattered around.

"Go away?" Daddy said. He folded up the table after Mama took off the cloth. "How far can they go when he doesn't have a car?"

"He's got Elmo's." Mama packed the tablecloth in the box with the punch bowl and clean cake plate.

"Does Elmo know?" Daddy looked at Uncle Elmo's back on the piano bench. He and Lester were doing a "Chopsticks" duet now.

"Well . . . no," Mama said, "but that will still leave him with the truck."

"Why couldn't the happy couple take the truck?"

"Harriet and I discussed this"—Mama pinched in her mouth—"but we decided nobody should have to start their married life going on a honeymoon in a Futty's Plumbing truck."

"Why not?" Daddy said. "When it's free."

"It rattles so," Mama said.

"So does a tin can." Daddy grinned.

"Now, what is that supposed to mean?" she asked. But he had turned away and was going out to get a picture of the honeymooners as they "went away."

Emmie Lou Ledbetter held my Bible while I helped chase kids away from the kitchen door after we ran out of Kool Aid. She thought I was Frances Anne when I came back and handed me the Bible. "Now honey," she said, "you just read every word and you'll never have any troubles you can't handle." She patted my hand. "Commit to memory all the verses you can. Why, there are sometimes I don't know what I'd do if I couldn't say a little Bible verse or two when things go wrong. And honey, they will. They will. Life is like that."

The preacher hooked his arm through hers and pulled her away. I let them out the back door. All the kids were in the front yard now, waiting for Frances Anne and Leon to leave.

Frances Anne stood in the doorway and everybody clapped. She did look pretty. Her hair was long and combed and curled. She wore a green linen suit the color of a January pine and a yellow print blouse with a bow tied at her neck. She took off her white corsage—Aunt Harriet's silk orchid from Easter—and threw it. Aunt Harriet's shoulder jerked a little. I knew she planned to wear that corsage next Easter and the next and the next.

"She's not supposed to do that," Mama frowned. "Only her bouquet. What happened to it?"

"Sudie put it in water," Aunt Harriet whispered. "I told her there were more flowers where those came from, but she did it anyway."

Aunt Harriet had made Frances Anne's bouquet from Queen Anne's lace and some paper doilies she had in the drawer with white gift wrap ribbon streamers.

The corsage landed in the shrubbery hedge and yellow-jackets flew out like sparks. Everyone jumped back. The kids ran.

Uncle Elmo stood beside his blue Plymouth. "I told Lester and his friends that the first one I saw with a bottle of white shoe polish or shaving cream would see more than the back of my hand." He said he'd washed his car yesterday and be durn if he was going to wash it again when they brought it back. "I don't have much finish left on that car," he said, "and shoe polish won't help."

He had let them tie balloons and crepe paper streamers on the doorhandles, radio antenna. While he wasn't looking somebody painted a big heart with initials and an arrow through it on the driver's side. The paint looked like the same rust-red Uncle Elmo had used on his porch last year.

Shorty came by in his Pepsi truck, stopped to wish Frances Anne and Leon "the best." He passed out Pepsi to show he wasn't a sore loser. Mama made us take ours to the refrigerator, but some of the kids started shaking theirs, held their fingers on the top, then let them spew out a Pepsi fight. That's when Aunt Harriet sent everybody home and asked Mama whatever in the world Frances Anne and Leon kept standing around when they had a honeymoon to go on and reservations at the Heart of Cottonville Motor Inn. She sent Uncle Elmo a hint by narrowing her eyes, saying, "I got supper to cook and a thousand things to do."

"Me too," Mama said. "I think we've done enough for one day. Sudie seemed to really appreciate it."

"She really seemed to enjoy it. She's got a good heart, even if she does try your patience at times. And, after all, what are neighbors for if not to help when there's a need?"

Uncle Elmo came back looking tired. "Leon says he can't drive. Never learned how."

"What?" Mama asked. "And of course Frances Anne can't drive either."

"We'll have to—" Aunt Harriet started.

"Don't look at me," Daddy said. He took the camera strap from around his neck, began to wind film. "Not me."

"I guess I'm elected," Elmo said. "I feel better about driving my car myself."

They left in a roar with a puff of exhaust. Everyone waved. Sudie stood beside Aunt Harriet, wiped her eyes. "My little girl is gone. I can't believe it. Why it seems like last week I plaited her hair in pigtails, waved her off to school."

"They grow up," Aunt Harriet said, "and we have to let go—get on with the rest of our lives. I've said that every time."

Sudie hugged them, thanked everyone over and over. "Nobody could ask for better neighbors. I just want you to know I appreciate it. Everything you did."

"We do what we can," Mama sighed. "I only wish we'd had more time . . . but everything turned out okay."

"Just fine," Daddy said. "You got the knot tied."

We walked home together. I changed clothes and went back to Nancy Drew, *Mystery of the Old Clock*. Getting married, I decided, was a lot of fuss with everybody all the way around and meant having to wear stiff clothes and tablecloths on your head.

Supper was late, but Mama had made an apple cobbler. "I was too tired to make crusts," she said. I helped with the dishes and didn't have to be asked.

"I made a cake and cobbler today," Mama said, "and there's not a crumb of either one left." She scrubbed the pan. "The rest of those apples go in the deep freeze as soon as I can get them there."

The whole family had to help peel and core, though Lester ate more than he peeled. We sat on the porch and joked, peeled apples until it was too dark to see. Daddy said if he turned on the lights it would attract bugs, so we finally stopped peeling and looked at stars. I wondered what Frances Anne and Leon were doing? If they saw the same stars. Probably they watched television. Frances Anne had certain shows she wouldn't miss for Mr. Anybody. Life or death.

We were almost ready to go inside when Sudie Gurley crept around the corner of the house. "Sudie!" Mama jumped. "You almost scared me to death. What's wrong?"

"I feel just lost.," Sudie held her hand over her heart. "That house is so quiet I can hear myself think. It's awful."

I heard Daddy give a little chuckle. "If you all are going to be out here awhile," he said at the door, "I'll turn on the lights, but I'm turning in. Tomorrow's another day."

"Good night," Mama said, then turned to Sudie. "I'm so tired, thunder couldn't keep me awake."

"What?" Aunt Harriet came across the street. "What's going on?"

Sudie told her. "Of course you are," Aunt Harriet said, "and having that empty apartment next door is enough to bring out the ghosts."

"A whole empty house." Sudie almost burst into tears. "I can't bear it."

"Surely there's somebody who can put you up for the night." Mama waved away a moth who had bumped the porch light, gotten stunned.

"You got sisters," Aunt Harriet told Sudie.

"You can't depend on them," Sudie said. "They wouldn't give me air if I was in a jug. Why, I couldn't call them about Frances Anne getting married. They wouldn't come or bring her any wedding gifts. My family never forgave me for marrying Grover Gurley. They all married *above*. I was the only one who married *beneath*. It hasn't been an easy life." Sudie twisted a handkerchief. It looked wet and limp. Like she'd been crying.

"Get your pajamas, May Kay," Mama said. "You can spend the night with Mrs. Gurley."

"But—" I started.

"Just once," Mama said tiredly, "for tonight."

I got my things, packed them in the plaid zippered bag my grandmother had given me for Christmas, and started to tuck in Nancy Drew when I remembered Frances Annne's bedroom and her stacks of romance magazines. I wouldn't need anything to read. I could close the door and leave the light on, read all night without anybody telling me to turn it out and go to sleep.

I helped Sudie change the sheets. By the time I got in bed and all settled down with *True Love* and *Secrets of Love,* it was nearly eleven o'clock. I read until after twelve. All the stories were alike. She loves him, he doesn't love her, they finally love each other. Or he loved her and so does his best friend. I turned out the light.

The next thing I knew I heard a noise that sounded like a scratch across a screen. Then whispering. Heads bobbed and shadows brushed across the window. I crept from bed, my heart leaping like a yoyo in my chest. Somebody was trying to break in Sudie Gurley's house! Robbers? A rapist? The floor creaked once under me and I froze. The voices stopped, then started again.

I ran across the living room, thankful the carpet muffled my feet. "Wake up." I shook Sudie Gurley. She lay curled in an oval like the old woman in the moon, her gray hair in a rope on top of the sheet. "There's somebody breaking in."

"Huh?" she said. "What?"

"They're breaking in Frances Anne's window." I shook her harder.

"Call the police." She had her eyes open now and rummaged under her pillow for a flashlight. She nearly knocked the telephone off the table reaching for the receiver, but she dialed the number in the dark, told them the address and hurry, there were two women alone in the house. (This was the first time I'd been called a woman and it made feel two inches taller, my arms stronger.)

Sudie got a broom from the kitchen. I took an oval framed portrait off the wall. I'd cream somebody with it if they came through the door. Wring them around the neck.

We heard more noises, the screen being pulled, scraped against the house. Then somebody said "ouch" and "dammit." I wanted to call my daddy, to run home and get him, but my legs wouldn't work.

We waited behind the living room door. The thumps got louder. "They're in the house," I whispered.

"Lord," Sudie said, "I wish I had a gun. I wish I had a gun."

I shook. Where was Mop? Why hadn't he barked? The dog had gone to sleep on his rug in the living room when I went to bed, but why didn't it bark. I knew. They had killed it. Poor little dog. The robbers had snatched Mop and choked it to death without a sound. Two of them against the two of us and I was only twelve. I'd spent my whole life growing up and just when I got ready to live it, somebody tried to kill me. No, I said inside. No. I saw shadows come closer. They would be through the door any minute. I held the picture higher. One, two, three . . . ready! I whanged it hard over the first burglar. "Oh," he hollered. "What the hell was that?"

Sudie flammed away with her broom and her robber finally held his hands up. "Don't. Stop. What's going on?" Then finally someone cried, "Mama." It sounded like Frances Anne being beaten there on the floor with the broom. "Mama! What's wrong with you? Don't you know who we are? Are you crazy?"

I turned on the lights and Sudie hugged Frances Anne and Leon, said she was sorry but we were scared half out of our minds. How had they gotten home?

"We took a taxi, Mama, what else?" Frances Anne said.

Then we heard the police car stop, saw lights flash blue and white in every window. They knocked. "Open up. It's the police."

Sudie flung open the door and two blue policemen burst into the room. "All right, fella." The taller one walked toward Leon. "Let's not have any trouble." He held handcuffs. Leon backed away.

"He's my son-in-law," Sudie said. "Wait."

"The police," Frankie said. "Mama, you called the police on your own daughter."

"I'm sorry, officers," Sudie said. "It's been a mistake. They were on their honeymoon and—"

"It's okay, lady," the pear-shaped policeman said, "as long as you know what you're doing."

"He's my son-in-law," Sudie said.

"He can be part of your family all you want," the policeman said, "but you need to get some things worked out." He let Leon go, looked at his partner, said, "I'm going to the car for a minute. Long as you got things under control here."

Frankie and Leon sat on the porch. She held Mop, half the time kissing him, half hugging him on her lap. You'd think she'd been gone from that dog a dozen years the way she acted. Leon just looked at the wall.

"Mama," Frankie said, "you embarrass me to death."

The remaining policeman took out a pencil and tried to scribble in his notebook, reached in his pocket for a penknife, and sharpened his pencil.

Sudie watched pencil shavings dust down to her floor.

"You people need the name of a counselor?" the policeman asked.

"We only got married yesterday," Frankie said, kissing the dog. "We've never had a fight. Except this one. And that's just Mama. She gets scared of anything that moves in the night."

The second policeman came to the door, called his partner out. "Excuse me for a minute," he said. "I'll be right back. In the meantime see if you can't work things out among yourselves."

"I feel faint," said Sudie, laying her hand like a white feather across her forehead.

I went to the kitchen for a glass of water, hurried, sloshing a trail behind me as I ran back. All this was too good to miss.

"Mama," Frankie said, "you have embarrassed me all my life."

Leon looked at his toes like he was seeing them for the first time. Hangdog, was what Mama and Aunt Harriet would call it. He had a hangdog look. I don't know that he ever had anything else, but at that moment, I thought he'd just disappear, get as invisible as a ghost, if he had the power, which he didn't, so he just stared at his scuffed old tennis shoes like they had writing on them.

Frankie tucked the dog under her arm, flounced into her bedroom, and slammed the door so hard the house rocked. We heard the lock click like a final word.

Then a knock on the front door. A knock from someone who knew how to do it. One of the policemen. "Ma'am," he said, "we got a problem."

Sudie handed him her glass of water, but he refused it. "My partner—he's got this memory for faces and he thinks this Leon fellow here looks like somebody he's seen before. We'd like to take him in—nothing official—just a friendly little visit downtown to see if there's anything we need to talk about. If that's okay with you."

"No." Frankie lunged from the door. She'd been listening all the time, and she made a bear hug for Leon. "I won't let you go."

Leon gave a half smile, shrugged. He'd never been in such demand, had so much attention in his life. He eased toward the door the policeman held.

"I won't let them keep you," Frankie yelled, grabbed his arm, tried to pull him back. "I mean it. I'll break that jail down."

"Nobody said anything about jail, lady," said the policeman. "We're just going to have a cup of coffee and talk about some things. Real nice like."

Frankie grabbed the policeman's hat from the TV where he'd laid it earlier, flung it at him. "You want to ruin my honeymoon. The only one I'll ever have."

"It takes all kinds," the policeman said. "If there's one thing I've learned in this business . . . it take all kinds."

Mop crawled from under the piano and barked like he'd been stepped on.

Frankie picked up the dog, buried her face in its fur, wiped her nose, and sniffled. "I'll never forgive you for this, Mama," she said, "as long as I live." She slammed her door again.

I wondered where I was going to sleep the rest of the night. Maybe I could sit on the steps, still warm from the tracks of Leon and the policeman, and wait until day walked in.

Sudie gulped the last of her water. "May Kay." She fastened me tight to one spot with her command. I'd never heard her speak so directly before. "You are not going to say one word about this night to your mama or daddy or Harriet or Elmo or anybody for the rest of your life. Hear me?"

I said I heard her. I didn't say what I would tell and what I wouldn't.

She made a bed on the couch for me. I tried to read the rest of Nancy Drew, but fell asleep sometime before dawn looked in the glass on the door. The minute I woke and realized where I was, I couldn't wait to get home. First, I had to tell Mrs. Gurley that I enjoyed spending the night. Which was a lie. I hadn't enjoyed it. I surely never wanted another like it in my life. Did it all happen?

Sudie Gurley thumped in the kitchen. "Sit down," she said.

I sat.

She rolled piecrust, lifted it like a paper plate into the pie dish, then fluted it like a sculptor, turning and pinching, turning and pinching. Mama always said her pies were works of art if they did take all day to make them. I waited.

She poured in cherry filling, laid on the top crust. It had a design of stems and leaves and cherries.

"I've always thought fresh pie made the nicest breakfast in the world," she said. She wore an apron so white it hurt, with ruffles crisp as the crust. Her hair, in twisted braids, rode her head like a crown.

I knew I had to stay for breakfast or hurt her feelings.

The clock ticked.

I watched the pie bubble and brown in the oven.

Sudie Gurley made a regular path to Frankie's door and back. She begged a dozen times to please come out. She tried to bribe her with pie. She said she'd forget everything that happened.

There was only silence.

I couldn't believe all I'd seen. The Police! The Police had been over at the Gurleys' in the middle of the night and hauled Leon off.

"Good Lord," Mama said. "The police? I was tired enough to sleep through thunder, but looks like I'd have heard some of all that going on."

I think she was upset because she missed the excitement or maybe she felt the neighborhood was no longer safe if she didn't have an eye and ear alert to anything out of the ordinary.

Aunt Harriet said she never for a minute had seen what Frances Anne saw in that Leon and if Sudie had thought twice she would have stopped the whole thing before it got started good.

"That's that," said Mama as though she dusted her hands and her mind of the whole affair and was ready to be on to the next thing.

Three months later I heard Mama and Aunt Harriet in the kitchen and something in their tone made me ease closer. When I stumped my toe on the Queen Anne leg of the huntboard and only made a small bump, they immediately stopped talking. Then Aunt Harriet started in about the Christmas bazaar and how she was the only one crocheting a thing for it. Everybody else would wait until the last minute, end up with felt and glue things that never had sold and never would and why did they vote to have a bazaar if they didn't intend to make something for it?

They had been talking about Frankie. I'd heard that much.

And how she was showing already. Maybe that's why they'd been in such an all-fired hurry to get the wedding going in the first place.

"If I'd known that," Aunt Harriet said, "I wouldn't have had any part of it. Not the first part."

"Yes, you would," Mama said, "and you know it. At times like this you have to think of the future and those innocent. We can't let them suffer the rest of their lives for something they couldn't help. Something beyond their control that happened before they were born."

Next thing I kew Aunt Harriet was crocheting baby booties and matching cap and carriage robe. "Not that it will ever have such a thing as a carriage," she said, "not with a daddy in jail, a mama that don't know the first thing about babies and where they come from and what they need when they get here." The booties weren't for the bazaar. She crocheted Christmas ornament bells for that and white snowflakes that she starched and spread on her kitchen table to dry. Or had in years past. This year everything she crocheted was blue.

"You act like you're going to be its grandmother instead of Sudie Gurley," Mama said.

They talked about it in front of me now as though I'd known it all along. I knew more than they thought but not as much as I wanted to.

Aunt Harriet looped blue wool around her little finger and said, "I know my Christian duty doesn't lie in some foreign country with strangers I'll never see, when someone right here on this street needs help."

In February they gave Frances Anne a baby shower, again baking cakes and making her a corsage by stuffing little socks with cotton, tying them with ribbons. They invited everybody they knew whether Frances Anne or Sudie knew them or not.

"You reckon any of Sudie's sisters will come?" Mama asked, wrapping the receiving blankets she'd bought.

"I'd faint in the front door if they did," Aunt Harriet said.

She wiped her icing spatula with two fingers then licked them. "I know white looks better, but everybody likes chocolate. And you've got to admit"—she took the batter bowl from me—"this is not your ordinary baby shower."

"Not with the daddy in prison and the mama refusing to say the baby's even due." Mama set her lips in a straight line.

"Sudie said Frankie felt it might be bad luck."

"Bad luck! I've heard every superstition to do with anything all my life and I've never heard that one," Mama said. "That's one of the first things anybody always asks—when's the baby due."

"Well, Frances Anne has always been funny about things."

"She gets it honest," Mama said, trying to fluff up her curly tie bow. "I bet she made up that bad luck business just to keep from having to lie."

"Lie?" I said. "What about?"

Mama cut her eyes at me, said sharply, "Premature babies that come into this world weighing ten pounds that's what."

I knew the subject was closed.

March came and went, so did April. Mama and Aunt Harriet kept counting on their fingers. "I don't think she's ever going to have it," Aunt Harriet said.

"I've heard of ten-month babies," Mama said. "This could be one of those."

I hadn't seen Frankie in months. "What does she do with herself?" Mama asked Aunt Harriet once.

"Reads, watches TV."

"Anybody watches TV that much, looks like they'd go blind or crazy one," Mama said, "which ever came first."

We had Easter and I got my first shoes with one-inch heels. I was on my way to being grown-up.

"I hate to see it," Aunt Harriet said when I tried them on for her. "Next thing we know she'll be like Frances Anne Gurley."

"Over my dead body," Mama said. I figured she really meant my dead body first.

The second day of May in the middle of the morning

Frances Anne had the baby before the taxi could get her to the hospital. "In the car," Mama whispered. "Curt Cleveland says he'll have to have the whole seat reupholstered."

"Just think," Aunt Harriet said, "if I'd been home instead of at the circle meeting, I would have taken her and my car would have gotten it instead."

"You read about things like this in the newpaper or see them on television, but you never think of them happening right in your own neighborhood," Mama said.

Frankie had a girl she named Diana Lee. Lee was her daddy's middle name.

Aunt Harriet and Mam both counted on their fingers and the baby had been born nine months to the day after the wedding. "It could have been late," Mama said, trying to swallow all their months of speculation. "First babies usually are by two weeks."

But Aunt Harriet said no, this time she thought the calendar and the marriage ceremony were in direct line. And that was something. If it had to be, it had to be and we must not hold it against the baby even if she did have those same criminal little eyes just like her daddy.

"If she's raised right," Mama said, "maybe it can be got out of her."

"We'll have to do all we can," Aunt Harriet said. "And if Sudie and Frances Anne won't take that baby to church, I will. I mean it," she said, "as soon as it's old enough."

Mama opened her mouth to say something, then stopped and quietly closed it.

Neither of them ever got a chance to raise Frankie's baby "right." When it was six weeks old, Grover Gurley came driving up one day in a ten-year-old Lincoln the color of a canary and packed everything they could into it. A van he'd hired followed behind. They moved to Tryon, North Carolina, where he'd bought a farm. "Plantation," Sudie giggled, put her hand over her mouth when she said it. She almost clapped her hands when she told Mama and Aunt

Harriet. "There's almost fifty acres and it has barns and horses and—"

Daddy said Grover must have won it *off* somebody or got in with the mob. He probably wouldn't have it long.

But he did. All of them came back to visit—Sudie, Frankie, and the baby. She had dark hair, and blue eyes round as chicory blooms. She laughed, played pattycake. I held her warm and soft against me, pushed the porch swing back and forth.

"She seems a bright little thing," Aunt Harriet said after they left.

"She doesn't take after the daddy then," Mama said, snapping the first beans from the garden. "I never trusted that man's eyes."

Daddy put his paper down. "Grover Gurley told me he quit gambling the minute he got that farm."

Uncle Elmo laughed, "He's really gambling now. Whether he knows it or not."

Since then there have been two families in and out both sides of the duplex where the Gurleys had lived. Aunt Harriet's piano stayed. She used to mention moving it back and Daddy and Uncle Elmo would both groan. "You want it done, you hire it," they said. "Once was enough for us."

So she hushed. "Nobody played it anyway."

"I just hope whoever lives there appreciates it," Mama said. "It was such a lovely wedding."

"Even if it didn't last," Aunt Harriet said.